Sister Karol's

MW00466048

"Whether you are a novice or, like me, have been a lifelong practitioner of folk magic, *Sister Karol's Book of Spells, Blessings & Folk Magic* by Karol Jackowski will feed your heart and soul in a way and in places you didn't even know were starving. It is the book I have been craving and searching for forever, and I am so grateful that she wrote it. In the first part of her divine, inspired book, you will feel Sister Karol's spirit with you as she gently calls you back to the God within us all. In our busy mundane lives, it is so easy to place our spirituality on the back burner. Novices will be gently introduced to straightforward practical ways on how to approach and create their own spirituality and how to incorporate it into their daily lives. As a more experienced practitioner, the first part of Sister Karol's book helped me to call back all the scattered pieces of myself and refocus my spiritual practice. The real gift her book gave me however is confirmation that there are other people like me–a sense of belonging to a solitary practitioner. The second part of her book contains beautiful spells, blessings, prayers, and folk magic from numerous religious traditions. Many I already know, and it felt like coming home, but so many were new and exciting to me, and it felt like a new adventure! This is a beautiful, sacred, and important book that I look forward to sharing with everyone I know." –Mary-Grace Fahrun, author of *Italian Folk Magic: Rue's Kitchen Witchery*

"Here are spiritual recipes, complete with instructions to conjure the best in any situation life throws at you. Whether you need the magic of belief, the antidote for snark, or blessings for abundance, Sister Karol has the cure. Witty and wise, this is magic for all folks, great and small, and anyone who knows a Godwink when they see one." –Adriana Trigiani, bestselling author of *Tony's Wife*

"If you are a witch who calls on the saints like I do, you will fall in love with *Sister Karol's Book of Spells, Blessings & Folk Magic*. It is a book of magic, yes, but written by a woman steeped in the ritual and lore of Catholicism. Sister Karol shows us what a life of prayer can look like, gives the reader practical magical advice, and reminds us that spirits want to visit us, too. It's not just us reaching out to them, but them reaching in. You can read the book straight through or read it as needed, like many spell books. She's giving us more than mere instruction though. Sister Karol writes from a mystical heart. It's a grimoire of love. After finishing it, I couldn't wait to get home to my altar."
–Aliza Einhorn, author of *The Little Book of Saturn*

For those who believe that a Catholic nun would have no idea or concept regarding the intricacies of magical spellwork, think again! From setting up magical altars to dressing candles, working with incense, and reciting magical prayers, Sister Karol has captured and presented what I believe to be the Catholic version of Hoodoo. Based on religious beliefs, many people avoid practicing

magic because they fear spiritual consequences, convinced that it is "sinful" to do so. Well, fear no more! *Sister Karol's Book of Spells, Blessings & Folk Magic* provides numerous spells including those for gambling, money drawing, love drawing, ancestor work, and even binding your enemies–all in a context that is not only untainted from iniquities, but also teaches us to work them alongside God and the Holy Deities. Prayers are basically magical incantations, and Sister Karol teaches us how to implement these incantations provided to us in the Holy Bible, alongside our altar work. I'm so excited and can't wait to incorporate many of Sister's Karol's spells into my own practice! This book is phenomenal!"
–Miss Aida, author, psychic, Hoodoo practitioner, and Catholic Spiritualist, *www.MissAida.com*

"Sister Karol's Book of Spells, Blessings & Folk Magic is a wonderful little book that looks at prayer, belief, and miracles through a new lens. Sister Karol, a Roman Catholic nun, embraces all religions and spiritualities, without judgment, by giving us the tools to find the 'magic' in our lives through prayer and ritual. In this way, she takes down the boundaries between us, and she makes it fun! As she interchanges words to reach all people, we are meant to see the similarities between belief systems. She implores us to be positive and believe in the magic that comes from knowing that 'wishes' really do come true. Sister Karol shows us that prayer is not just articulation of words but also includes living and following with creating rituals and altars that bring God into our lives constantly. Our life is a prayer. Abracadabra . . .

Amen." –Anna Raimondi, author of *Conversations with Mary: Messages of Healing, Hope, and Unity for Everyone*

"*Sister Karol's Book of Spells, Blessings & Folk Magic* by Karol Jackowski is a pleasant surprise. Having been raised Roman Catholic myself, I recognized immediately how Sister Karol has crafted a blend of workings loosely based on the order of Catholic ritual and the use of Catholic sacramentals with her own creativity drawn from other sources of inspiration. If the magical side of the Christian faith is appealing to you, you will find a very workable system here with everything needed. Sister Karol has written her *Book of Spells* in such a manner that, even if you are new to magical work, you will have no problem getting positive results. The secret is your intention and application of what Sister Karol teaches you within these pages"
–C. R. Bilardi, author of *The Red Church or the Art of Pennsylvania German Braucherei* and *Wapallopen, Luzerne County: A Forgotten Pennsylvania Dutch Enclave*

"*Sister Karol's Book of Spells, Blessings & Folk Magic* is a luminous source of wisdom and inspiration. There is something for everyone and every occasion: from baby blessings to wedding ceremonies, spells for real estate, true love, and safe travel as well as timeless prayers. Keep it close by, for like a beloved companion, you will return to it often." –Virginia Bell, astrologer and author of *Midlife Is Not a Crisis: Using Astrology to Thrive in the Second Half of Life*

"This gift of Karol Jackowski's wisdom, spirit, energy, and hope arrives with perfect timing in a world that desperately needs these recipes for creation of holy magic in our hearts, homes, and beyond. I also greatly cheer the added bonus of the chance to sink into yet another rich work by this fascinating writer and woman. Those with–or even without–a crumb of religiosity or spirituality are sure to find a new guru and best friend" –Suzanne Strempek Shea, award-winning author of *Sundays in America, Make a Wish But Not for Money*, and other books

"There are many who have written about magic and folklore, but not many of these books have been written by a nun. Karol Jackowski has created a way to unearth a familiar, ancient sense of true esoteric faith, reminiscent of a way of life once lived before the modern world took hold. Karol's knowledge of saints and diverse traditions is impeccable and her practice of magic powerful. With each page, you can almost taste the essence of sacred light flowing out from within her words. The perception of a nun's monastic life leads one to conjure thoughts of hermetic days enclosed in strict confinement of spiritual views, but Karol breaks all the misconceptions and barriers and illuminates a path we have all longed for deep inside ourselves. This book is a revelation, as *Sister Karol's Book of Spells, Blessings & Folk Magic* is an invitation to re-embrace our world as a sacred form of magic in itself. Weaving between blessings for babies, sacred prayers, purifications, and altar work, there is something for everyone to draw upon and immerse into their daily life.

This is a powerful companion for inner mystics to steer their heart's compass to the divine in life." –Andrés Engracia, author of *Saints and Mystics Reading Cards*

"Open *Sister Karol's Book of Spells, Blessings & Folk Magic*, and you will open your heart to possibility and connection. You'll also be prepared to welcome new babies, bless your pets, and celebrate your birthday with your spirit guides. Sister Karol delivers holiness with a smile and a wink, offering practical magic with a divine assist. Warning to readers: this book will cast a joyful spell on you." –Kate Whouley, author of *Remembering the Music, Forgetting the Words*

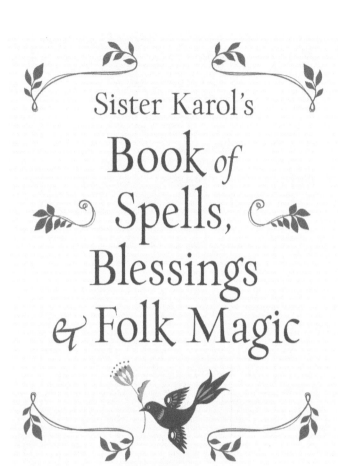

Sister Karol's
Book *of*
Spells,
Blessings
& Folk Magic

KAROL JACKOWSKI

WEISER
BOOKS

This edition first published in 2019 by Weiser Books, an imprint of
Red Wheel/Weiser, LLC
With offices at:
65 Parker Street, Suite 7
Newburyport, MA 01950
www.redwheelweiser.com

All scripture quotes have been paraphrased from
the *New American Bible* (1970).

ISBN: 978-1-57863-645-7
Library of Congress Cataloging-in-Publication Data available upon request.
Cover and text design by Kathryn Sky-Peck
Typeset in Incognito
Printed in Canada

MAR
10 9 8 7 6 5 4 3 2 1

CONTENTS

part two

SPELLS, BLESSINGS, AND FOLK MAGIC

PREFACE

*Y*ou might be wondering how a nun got interested in spells and magic. You might also be surprised to learn that it happened quite naturally, fitting perfectly into everything that I learned and believed in, growing up Catholic. I was born and raised believing in God, angels, saints–a spirit-filled world in which we had the ability to talk to them, ask for whatever we needed, and sense a divine presence with us wherever we were. At Saint Stanislaus Grade School in East Chicago, Indiana, we attended Mass every morning before class, where we watched a priest transform bread and wine (in the mysterious language of Latin) into the body and blood of Christ. Abracadabra. Catholic magic. I grew up thinking if bread and wine could be transformed into something divine, so could the rest of creation. The holiness in all creation can be found in those who have eyes to see what they believe.

In 1984, I moved to New York City to begin doctoral work at New York University–a city unlike any other on the face of this earth, where diversity is treasured as its heart and soul, and

I ended up celebrating everyone's holidays and holy days because they were my neighbors and friends. I celebrated Hanukkah, Yom Kippur, and Rosh Hashanah with Jewish friends, and solstices and equinoxes with Wiccan neighbors. We all celebrated the same times of year in different ways, recognizing the holiness in the food we ate, the seasons of the year, and the love we shared, which transformed everything into moments we'd never forget. I found more in common with different religious beliefs than disconnected, feeling enriched by the differences, making many my own. That's when my interest in spells and magic became part of me in ways that only grow deeper.

Wanting to write a book on spells, blessings, and folk magic was born from my interest in what we all believe, and my desire to find ways we can cherish and revere as holy the beliefs of others who know a different experience of God. I wanted to find ways to bring us together at a time when so many forces threaten to tear us apart. I believe in one God who reveals divinity in different ways to different people, with all ways equally divine, none truer than others. There are as many paths to God as there are people who walk this earth, and not all of them lead to church.

In this book, I talk about what my life of prayer looks like, what I do, and how it works to help me–in the words of Saint Richard of Chichester–"see more clearly, love more dearly, and follow more nearly" the inner voice I hear to help bring joy into the world. I collected all my favorite spells, blessings, and folk magic recipes, the prayers most effective in granting my wishes, and I give them to you here. My wish is that you, the soulful reader, will see more clearly how everything is holy, just as it is, and how we are all called to revere and celebrate the divine life in all creation.

My hope is that you love reading this book as much as I loved writing it, and that it may become a prayer book for you, as it is for me. My greatest hope is that you might even consider making your own prayer book of spells, blessings, and folk magic because our world needs all the love and joy we can put out there. Mostly I pray this book grants you peace.

BLESSED BE

Part One

IN THE
BEGINNING

*T*his book is about prayer and how important ritual becomes at certain times in our lives. Those who've grown up in ancient religious traditions–Judaism, Pre-Christian, Catholicism, Buddhism, Islam–know instinctively the powerful way ritual prayer blesses every moment of every day. At its very best, religion teaches us to revere everything as holy, just the way it is. Even those who are decidedly not religious in the traditional sense occasionally feel the need for divine intervention, blessing, and inspiration, especially in life's most profound turning points like birth, marriage, sickness, and death. They too believe in the power of prayer to help good things happen, bring comfort in times of sorrow, enlighten next steps when we feel lost and confused. As a matter of fact, the fastest growing "religion" today is giving birth to a new kind of "*none*," those living at the heart of what the Dalai Lama sees as a spiritual revolution, a shift in consciousness touching the heart of those who seek to save their soul without religion. This book is written with everyone in mind, especially "*nones.*"

Who are these "*nones*"? "*Nones*" are those who find divine inspiration not in organized religion–which increasingly appears to be a divisive source of hatred, discrimination, and violence–but in a level of profound concern about one's own spiritual life and the well-being of others. These "*nones*" are also missionaries of peace on earth and resisters of injustice. At their very best, they bow before the divinity in all creation. While "*nones*" may hold in contempt the God of organized religion made in the image and likeness of their believers, more importantly they appear drawn singleheartedly to a sacred presence in all of life that surrounds, inspires, and guides, felt as soulful, and experienced as divine. The call these "*nones*" hear to pray is deeply personal and the longing for ritual soulfully profound. At the deepest level of what it means to be human, I suspect we all share a desire at some points in life to live closer to our God. We feel called to pray. We all long to find heaven in all the hell on earth.

The spells, blessings, and folk magic in this book are for both believer and nonbeliever. There are favorite rituals and prayers for believers in God, Jesus, Mary, angels, and saints, and there are what I fondly call spells and folk magic: home-made prayers and rituals for those who see holy spirits present in nature, neighbor, and the ordinary events of daily life. Because none are mutually exclusive, in all of these spells and blessings you'll find both–the soulfully personal mixed with the deeply traditional–potentially the most powerful prayer of all. When we mix matters of the heart with spiritually charged rituals, divine intervention occurs. We make magic.

Long before religion became organized in churches and its powers centralized exclusively in men, practicing religion at home was the norm, most likely led by women. Every household had its deities, its altars, its daily rituals, with meals most sacred, sources of Holy Communion. All of life became part of ritual prayer. Ancient religious texts are full of household spells, blessings, and folk magic for the most ordinary things, such as healing a foot, silencing a barking dog, preventing snakebite, having a good singing voice–and a personal favorite–making a man tongue-tied. At first, some concerns appeared trite and unworthy of divine attention, until I read on to see how sacred ordinary life was to our earliest ancestors. All of life was holy, charged with the presence of God, and everything became sacred for those who knew how to see. These commonplace rituals became folk magic for the soul, all meant to strengthen our connection to the divine mysteries of everyday life. Everything came with a purpose; everything became part of life's mystery. Those are the good old days. Connecting daily to what is holy in heaven, on earth, and in one another is an ancient soul-saving grace.

Roman Catholicism preserved the primitive instinct in finding everything holy by assigning saints and angels very specific duties responding to every human need. For example, Saint Lucy specializes in curing eye problems. Veronica is the patron saint of laundry. Teresa of Avila, the sixteenth-century mystic, became the advocate for writers and reliever of migraine headaches. Saint Dymphna, patron of those suffering mental illness, is also known to protect from those who drive us crazy. Saint Clare is the patron saint of television; Saint Francis of Assisi, the protector of animals; and Saint Joseph, most famous for buying or selling new homes (if you bury his statue upside down in the backyard). If you can't find something you fear lost, Saint Anthony is your man. *"Beloved Saint Anthony, please come around. Something's lost and can't be found."* I'm not the only one who still attests to the fact Saint Anthony never fails to find what's lost. Even non-Catholic friends testify to Saint Anthony miracles. Few things feel more miraculous than lost items found.

In addition to a communion of saints, I grew up surrounded by angels, still believing that at birth we're all assigned a guardian angel who helped prepare our soul for this lifetime, a spirit guide, remaining at our side forever. In Saint Stanislaus Grade School, nuns even instructed us to scoot over at our desks, making room for our guardian angel. While that advice felt more like divine incentive to behave, I still feel an angel at my side always, at least one. The divine point in all these beliefs reveals everything is holy just as it is, and maintaining a connection with divine spirits throughout the day grants peace. We really can, in thought and deed, find heaven in all the hell on earth. We can make wishes come true.

There's no official explanation of why the earliest pre-Christian prayers were known as spells, except for the primitive belief that's exactly what deities do when we call–stop by for a spell. The spell itself has everything to do with God's visit and what happens when divine intervention occurs. Those who pray in ordinary ways do so in times of crisis as well as with the simplest matters of everyday life. Because rituals come from the soul, they are naturally, supernaturally, experienced as divine, full of grace, full of magically favored moments. Lives are changed by such mysterious activity. Even if we don't get what we want immediately, something happens, and what we want to happen gradually becomes real. That's the power in spells and therein lies the magic. When deities stop by for a spell, something changes in us; we somehow feel better. We may not know what happened, but we feel noticeably different after prayer, lifted up and calmer, with what Buddhists call "evenness of mind." In ways we don't understand completely, prayer blows a little wind beneath our wings and we feel better. Abracadabra.

In the 1970s, I felt drawn to the rituals, spells, and folk magic of ancient Pagan and Wiccan traditions, finding myself comfortably at home. As Catholics, we also celebrate the winter solstice with Christmas, and spring equinox with Easter. The use of water, incense, oils, fire, candles, and vestments was familiar to me in Catholicism, as was the timing of our holiest days with the seasons of the year and phases of the moon. Our most sacred rituals are celebrated at life's most profound turning points: birth, marriage, sickness, death, forgiveness, initiation into adulthood, ordination into priesthood. I looked at ancient spells in which candles and incense were burned and ritualistic activities repeated for three, seven, or nine days for effectiveness and saw Catholic novenas repeated for three, seven, or nine days as well. I saw *repetition* revealed as a sacred ingredient in prayers being answered and spells making magic. Repeating rituals celebrated for thousands of years opens the door to the most divinely charged activities of all. That is why Catholicism reveres the Eucharist–commemorating the Last Supper–as its most sacred ritual, uniting believers in the Body of Christ. In pre-Christian rituals, calling on the divine energy present in all of nature–heaven and earth–becomes the magic ingredient in summoning divine intervention. Tuning into a world charged with the presence of God is what we do when we enter into ritual prayer with spells, blessings, and folk magic. We open the door to divine intervention, and our lives are transformed in the process, granting us peace to bring to bear.

In growing up Catholic, I became possessed by an enchanted spiritual life, born and raised with a mysterious vision of this world. Long before the age of reason (believed to be seven years old), we learned from nuns and priests–God's representatives–about a three-in-one God, made up of a Father, a Son, and a Holy Spirit (known for years as a Holy Ghost), the most mysterious of the three. I grew up believing in ghosts and spirits as divine, sources of everlasting goodness in this world. There was also Mary, Mother of God, Mother of Jesus, spouse of Saint Joseph, and our spiritual Mother. We had family in heaven and on earth. Following the Holy Family were choirs of angels, Cherubim and Seraphim, and a communion of saints, one whose name we were given in baptism, as a spirit guide and personal advocate. We entered this life well-equipped spiritually, knowing we were never alone. We saw how thin the veil is between this world and the spirit world, and how easily accessible it is when we pray; the door to the spirit world opens and we enter. Anytime and anywhere, holy spirits stood ready and willing to help when called upon. Mix all of the above together for a lifetime and it becomes you. Add to the mix the daily prayers and rituals in being a nun for over fifty years and it becomes you even more. At least it totally became me. So much so it now became this book. Abracadabra.

All the soulful questions asked and prayerful requests received make up this book. Rarely does a day go by when I don't receive requests for prayerful support. Like ancient folk magic, calls for prayerful assistance are as ordinary and diverse as passing a test, finding an apartment, healing the sick, comforting the grieving, selling a house, getting a job, binding those who hurt us. Some requests are speechless. The phone rings and friends ask, "Would you light a candle for me today?" Enough. They know. Most want to know the prayers and rituals I find helpful, as well as prayers to saints known to grant specific requests. Many are also drawn, as I am, to the prayers and rituals of other religious traditions as well. New York is the richest city in the world in giving its residents a consciousness of everyone's holidays and holy days, encouraging us to celebrate in spirit, realizing how we tend to celebrate in similar ways on certain days. We all light candles to illumine darkness. We burn incense with the hope of our prayer rising to heaven, repeating ancient prayers, litanies, novenas, chants, rituals, all charged and saturated with centuries of prayerful energy. Such are the spells and blessings found in this book. Something, it is hoped, for everyone. A ritual for every occasion.

Far more than just a little religious recipe book, here you'll also find everything needed to make your own *Book of Spells, Blessings, and Folk Magic*, the most important book of all. In *Part One: In the Beginning*, thought is given to understanding the impulse or "call" to pray; what prayer is, where it comes from, and what to do when we hear the call. Because creating sacred space is the first step, you'll also find described common elements of sacred spaces with encouragement to build your own home altars and shrines. Nearly all I know who hear the call to prayer also hear the call to create "home altars"; ordinary space made sacred where candles are lit, wishes made, and personal treasures collected–photos, crystals, statues, feathers, flowers, stones, seashells, urns of ashes from dearly departed loved ones, including pets. If you've been drawn to pick up this book, I suspect you already have at least one altar or shrine at home on top of a bookshelf, dresser, or table. You've already created sacred space at home for deities to stop by for a spell. This book is meant to find you.

At the heart of this book is an attempt to explain the magic in ritual and how divine power changes our lives; how to create magically favored moments in which miracles happen. Everything we experience, especially the worst of times, is capable of being transformed, even begs to be lived differently, with ritual prayer opening the door to divine intervention, to the grace of feeling better. Questions of where the power in ritual comes from as well as why, when, where, and how to ritualize prayer top the list. Here you'll find common magic-making elements in ritual prayer, as well as a seven-step process in creating your own spells and making your own magic. Step by step is how it happens; slow and steady is how the magic in ritual works. Making the invisible visible is what we do in ritual prayer. Out of the depths of the soul we call on deities for divine intervention and find revealed next steps, even if the next step is do nothing but wait. Clouds of unknowing are full of revelation for those who wait hopefully, and dark nights of the soul become enlightened, teaching how to see in the dark. Wherever we are in our life's journey is the stuff of magic; the holy place where transformation does its work. We bring our self to the altar, entering the spirit world just as we are, letting it be.

In *Part Two: Spells, Blessings, and Folk Magic,* you'll find old and new rituals for nearly every occasion. Some reflect ancient Christian rites; others draw on sacred rituals predating Christianity. Some are Roman Catholic in origin (but will work for all); Wiccan, Native American, and Jewish rituals are included as well. Valuable insights from nontraditional New Age experiences are also integrated. Some–like the "Ten-Cent Christmas Tree Blessing"(p. 155)–are pure and simple fun. All responded perfectly at one point in time to someone's prayerful request; all reveal the mystery and magic I find in the rituals of Catholicism, and all contain the pure joy and fun I know and love in rituals shared with family, sisters, and friends. Most importantly, all offer opportunities for you to taste and see for yourself how divine, how comforting, how mysterious, and how much fun ritual prayer can be.

The heartfelt prayer on every page of this book is for you, the prayerful reader, to begin here and now creating your own

Book of Spells, Blessings, and Folk Magic. Think about where and when you hear the call to solitude and prayer. How do you open your soul's door and get in touch with deities? How, when, and where do you experience divine activity? Look at the turning points in your life and see how you were transformed, or not. The soul is the place, the holy of holies, where all spells and blessings begin, where we folks begin to make magic. Ritual prayer is the sacred key in opening the soul's door and welcoming deities in for a spell; opening the door to divine intervention.

In the life of a writer, nothing is more sacred than blank pages waiting for words to appear. In the spirit of writing your own book, I encourage you to note favorite prayers and blessings. Add your own spells. Feel free to change the prayers and rituals in this book to suit your needs. Making rituals your own, as I have done here, is the most powerful magic of all. The thought of millions of *Books of Spells, Blessings, and Folk Magics* leads me to believe our world would be far less a mess if that happened. An endless flow of divine energy freeing compassion to work through the world is what's needed to make peace on earth. We are the magic stuff of miracles, put on earth in this lifetime to reveal, as did Christ, Buddha, and Muhammad, how divine it is to be fully human. We are all called to priesthood when we hear the call to prayer, called to be angels on earth who take religion into our own homes, hearts, and hands, and put our life on the altar.

Transforming into heaven all the hell on earth is what happens when we call on deities daily to stop by for a spell, praying to be guided in revering everyone as divine, seeing in everyone the face of God. Namasté. Divine intervention in daily life is all we need to see everything as holy, just the way it is. Everything comes with the purpose of transforming us into our best self, into divinely human stuff capable of changing the worst into the best of times. Ritual prayer, like personal prayer, is all we need to open the door to the spirit world and invite God in for a spell; all we need to make the magic of summoning divine intervention. In the end, I pray this *Book of Spells, Blessings, and Folk Magic* will do for you what it does for me—allow you to taste and see how divine this life can be, even in its darkest, most devastating, most confusing, and most mysterious moments. I pray this book grants you peace (and everything else you want).

*There is no day that
I do not hear
the Voice.*

– JOAN OF ARC

CALL TO PRAY

The call to pray feels mysterious and otherworldly at first because it speaks from something moving us profoundly, feeling as though we need divine intervention. We hear a voice call for help inside and out. Something touches us, moves us, devastates us, delights us, changes us, makes us laugh or cry, and a voice within calls us to respond. The more attention we pay to the inner voice–to what the Gospel of Mary Magdalene calls the "angel" in our soul–the more frequently we hear the call to pray, to speak and listen soulfully. We may feel called to pray for help, ask a favor, beg forgiveness, seek comfort, offer thanks, or sit speechless in silence. What makes prayer not so mysterious is how frequently we hear the call when we listen, and how ordinary our concerns feel. In hearing the call to pray, the manner is as ordinary as it is extraordinary. It's as ordinary as daily life, and extraordinary in that it opens the door to divine intervention.

The older I become, the more frequent and ordinarily a call to pray is heard, like daily bread. For example, whenever sirens scream on the streets of New York City, I call all angels to protect first responders and victims. In passing the sad, broken, and homeless on the street, I ask for divine intervention to help more than a few bucks for breakfast. Family and friends come to mind, and I hear a prayer for all manner of things to be well. Nearly every day someone appears who hears the call and wants to know what to do. Something happens, it doesn't take much, and the need arises for divine assistance, inspiration, protection, comfort, gratitude. Being called to pray is as ordinary as it is mysterious, heard by believer and nonbeliever alike, and in a language understood by all. Mysteriously ordinary.

The call to pray always feels completely mysterious to me, regardless of its frequency. The ordinary manner of the call enhances and magnifies the mystery. Early in Catholic education, we were told every twinkle in the starry starry night was a heartfelt prayer on its way to God, clear evidence trillions of people hear the call to prayer. That's how extraordinarily ordinary it is. We were also led to believe the end of this world would come when every star found its way to the divine resting place where all prayer is heard: God's lap. Every star a prayer. I still find myself believing that when every night one star passes through a piece of sky in the east window of my two-room apartment. Only one star–likely a planet–is visible in the night sky over New York City, leading me to believe this is a great spot for prayers being answered. The success rate appears exceptionally high (or the end is near). As far as I can see, we have only one big unanswered planet-size prayer left.

All of the above shows I'm clearly not alone in feeling the divine, primitive, soulful impulse we know to pray–whether it be to heal, console, get pregnant, get money, get a job, pass a test, celebrate an anniversary, sell a house, bind an enemy, get rid of a headache, or find true love–requests heard most often. In seeing how moved so many are to punctuate life's most stellar, most painful, most confusing, even most ordinary moments with prayer, I always feel my starry-eyed belief is not so silly. It's not just me, and it's not just a nun thing. Even those with no religious belief, for whom God is the Universe, kindness their religion, and compassion their Holy Spirit, even they feel moved to light candles and burn incense in response to what feels like a call to pray. It's not silly at all to see how simple prayers naturally feel like twinkling specks in the soul's dark night being drawn toward God. *"Such stuff as dreams are made on."*

Because the call to pray is as ordinary and personal as it is mysterious and divine, it's not difficult to see where it comes from. It's the stuff of everyday life that moves us to pray, stirring up feelings, making us sit up and take notice. Every day is our daily bread and our daily prayer. Something happens to confuse us, hurt us, delight us, and if we take care to listen before leaping, we naturally feel an impulse and hear the soul's call to wrap ourselves in solitude and pray. We pray to understand what's going on and how best to respond. We pause to listen before we leap. We take deep breaths and think twice before responding. We listen to inner voices in the dark and wait for next steps to be enlightened. Whenever we run into life's most sorrowful mysteries–accidents, natural disasters, illness, hatred, death–we are brought to our knees, plunged into the soulful depth of what always feels like speechless prayer. We are reduced to silence, a language only deities and angels understand. We pass through life's clouds of unknowing–the land of neither here nor there–feeling suspended in mid-air with nothing to lean on, praying for grace to let it be. The moment of greatest grace always lies in taking care to listen, in keeping still when we feel overwhelmed, waiting in the dark nights of our soul for dawn. Such soulful stillness is essentially full of grace–insight–because it helps in seeing more clearly what's happening, revealing what to do next, even if next steps point toward doing nothing, endowing us with the sanctifying grace to let it be.

In the beginning, the call to prayer moves us to stop, look, and listen for the still, small voice, for some insight and understanding into what's happening. Everything that happens bears a message we need to hear, a lesson we need to learn, begging us to see how everything is holy just as it is. The soul's ticket to entering all of life's mysteries lies in keeping still and remaining calm–maintaining "evenness of mind"–the key in opening the door to divine intervention. All who hear the call to pray see a divine opportunity to nourish more profoundly the capacity for good things to happen at a time when we couldn't feel worse. Prayer's purpose is not to influence God but to transform us, lift our spirit, and grant whatever we need to feel better. Prayer calls us to be mediums of love and compassion. We all have the soulful ability to shape fate by the choice to become loving and just or hateful and divisive. What we do with what life gives us is the most fateful act of all. At any given moment, we either lift one another up or put one another down. We choose to be kind and generous or mean-spirited and selfish. We choose to see clearly or turn away and ignore. Everything we do serves to create either heaven or hell on earth. Making the best out of the worst of times is what we're called to do when we hear the call to prayer. When we cry out for divine intervention, we are crying out for the grace to become better than how awful we feel. When we hear the soulful call to pray, we hear our best self–the angel in our soul–begging us to rise and shine. In hearing the call to prayer, we open our life to divine intervention and the endless possibility of finding heaven in all the hell on earth.

Call to Ritual Prayer

The call to ritual prayer is a way of connecting to ancient activities charged with thousands of years of divine energy. While we speak of ritual as prayerful activity, our lives are full of rituals that appear to have little or nothing to do with religion. Rituals are ordinary activities repeated over and over, often on the same date, at the same time, because that's what we love to do; that's how we remember and celebrate the most important days of our life, and that's how we get through every day the best we can. For example, if my day doesn't begin with the morning ritual of coffee, donut or Danish, news, and at least an hour of meditation and writing, envisioning the day to come, the rest of the day feels noticeably "off." The day isn't necessarily worse as a result, just slightly more mindless, not fully connected, not completely plugged in. Because this morning ritual has been part of my life for decades, when skipped, every cell in my body notices. More effort is needed on those days to pay attention, making the day more exhausting. That's how much ritual takes on a life of its own. That's how profoundly we need ritual to keep soul-fires burning. Even the most ordinary rituals–and best donuts–have everything to do with the care and feeding of the spiritual life. Soul food.

Holidays are times we experience how energizing ritual can be, often involving traditional elements of candle lighting, wish making, meals, parties, gift giving, gathering with loved ones. We instinctively mark life's most significant turning points–like birthdays and anniversaries–in ways we feel compelled to repeat year after year, so much so those days don't feel the same when the celebration is missed. Every time we repeat activities and continue rituals, the more meaningful they become, so much so they appear to take on a life of their own, becoming so meaningful we would not think of celebrating any other way. We bring to each ritual memories of past celebrations, often called to mind lovingly and enjoyed all over again. Year after year, rituals become more important, more meaningful, and more essential to what those days mean. Some rituals become so highly charged with energy experienced as divine that we cannot live happily without them. When rituals take on a life of their own, becoming soul food, they remain forever.

For many, the call to ritual prayer came early in life and never stopped calling. For those of us growing up Catholic, ritual prayer saturated our lives. The same is true for Jewish friends whose lives always shift gears soulfully to celebrate Yom Kippur, Rosh Hashanah, Hanukkah, Passover, and Friday night Shabbat. In addition to beginning every grade school day with Mass and Holy Communion, in Catholic high school and college, we also began and ended every class with prayer. Consciousness shifted in prayer, putting us in touch with God repeatedly throughout the day. Year after year, we learned more and more about the mystery and magic in ritual prayer. Along with higher and higher education, we also got higher and higher religion. All the ordinary Catholic rites and rituals became part of everything we did, eight hours a day, five days a week. That's why "lapsed" Catholics are first to admit how strange it is that some things never leave them. They still feel Catholic no matter how out of line they are with Church teaching. When it comes to spiritual development, some things become part of us forever. That's how powerful ritual prayer can be. Once enacted, ritual takes on a life of its own in us. Forever.

For example, nearly every Catholic I know, even the "lapsed," still treasures a secret heartfelt devotion to Mary, the Mother of God, thus the repeated reference to Mary in my favorite spells and blessings. Marian devotion was cultivated from the first day of Catholic education. I liked the idea of God having a Mother who visited children. In the early 1950s, we learned of children our age in Lourdes, France, being visited by Mary and receiving messages from her. We believed it could happen to us as well. Why not? We stared at statues of Mary waiting for her to cry, believing it could happen any time. We looked for messages in white envelopes. Catholicism was full of miracle stories happening to ordinary people, and that included us. We believed it all.

Devotion to Mary intensified at Saint Stanislaus Grade School, where all girls became members of the Children of Mary, a church-school club focusing on Marian devotion. More importantly, the group was devoted to teaching girls how divine it was to remain a virgin, until marriage or death. Even in the fifth grade, that was funny. All I remember about being a Child of Mary was processing into church on the first Sunday of the month robed in white and blue. Mini-Marys. We wore shin-length white capes with pale "Blessed Mother Blue" Peter Pan collars and blue felt beanies with a white satin *M* sewed on the front and a silky white string tassel on top. Because of the outfit and procession, we felt spiritually special, one of Mary's Girls. For many, devotion to Mary deepened over time, gradually transforming into a feeling of how divine it is to be a woman. Mission accomplished. Devotion to Mary in this book is as old as I am, here a gift for all. She never says no.

In discovering the mystery and magic in ritual prayer at an early age, we were also introduced to ritual's strangely power-ful ways and means of drumming up divine activity, of creat-ing magically favored moments. Rituals contained the divine power to effect what they signify. Bread and wine become Christ in us, body and blood, saturating our life with grace–the divine energy–to love. In confessing what we did wrong, we were forgiven every time. Sacred rituals were not confined to church alone though, with many brought home as well. Ours was a religion reaching beyond church into the homes of believers. Church rituals mixed with family rituals, making folk magic. As kids, we looked forward to one Polish ritual eagerly: the "Three Kings House Blessing"(p. 118). Every year, on January 6, feast of the Epiphany, the pastor and two altar boys visited everyone in the parish to bless homes and families at the beginning of the New Year. The ritual began with the priest knocking on the front door three times. It was very important not to keep him waiting, as though it would be a sin or bad luck if he had to knock three more times. Father entered the house first, wearing a floor-length gold cape, holding a small, black prayer book. Two altar boys followed: one holding an urn of holy water, white chalk, and white cloth, the other swinging the incensor back and forth. All three entered in a mysterious cloud of frankincense and myrrh. Such was the setting in which the "Three Kings House Blessing" took place.

The priest began reading a prayer of blessing on the family, giving us goosebumps. He incensed the four corners of the living room, sprinkling all (including dog, parakeet, and turtle) with holy water, making us laugh. With white cloth the priest wiped away last year's markings above the front door and wrote in its place with white chalk "K+M+B+1952"–first initials of the names of the Three Kings (Kaspar, Melchior, and Balthazar) plus the number of the New Year. That concluded the ritual and signaled time for a token of thanks. My mother slipped Father a small white envelope with a few bucks as they disappeared in a cloud of smoke to repeat the same ritual, house after house.

Much later, I learned every culture has its own version of a house blessing ritual, making it one of the most powerful rituals we know. Jewish friends nail a mezuzah inside the doorway–containing a passage from Jewish scripture–to bless all who enter the home. Catholic homes traditionally hung holy water fonts at the front and back door. Deities love to make themselves at home wherever we do, love to stop by for a spell, love to abide within, love to be part of the household and its activities, love to help us folks make magic. Deities live close to their people.

Many people have some little prayer space set aside, a self-made shrine or altar tucked privately in a corner or on a dresser top, usually tended to by the woman of the house. Some families build serious, high-maintenance yard shrines–with inverted bathtubs–usually tended to by the man of the house. We light candles to make wishes and cry for help. Sacred objects are gathered together and kept in a special place. All are clear indicators of how typical it is to take religion in our own hands, and how natural it is to engage in some kind of ritual prayer and whenever necessary, at our convenience.

Ritual prayer often becomes a simple, unnoticed, ordinary part of everyday life. In the spirit of our ancient ancestors, we too have household deities and altars, and practicing religion at home appears normal, not at all strange. Everybody I know does it. Religious rituals become mixed with family rituals, which become mixed with neighborhood life, becoming reflective of who we are. Elements of rituals–candles, incense, holy water, chanting, litanies, rosaries, bowed heads and bended knees, folded hands, extended hands, facing east–are mixed like a recipe to attain the desired effect. We know instinctively when the time calls for ritual prayer, and we have everything needed to open our home and invite deities in for a spell.

There are certain times in life that beg clearly for divine intervention and the powerful blessing rituals hold. Most religions celebrate and ritualize seven extraordinary times in life, seven of life's turning points worthy of the oldest, most powerfully divine rituals we know: Birth, Forgiveness, Communion, Adulthood, Marriage, Priesthood, and Sickness and Death. High holy rituals effecting what they signify. We are held together, sustained, enriched, and mystified by our rituals. Many experience early in life how mysterious, powerful, and life-changing rituals can be–even sacramental. At the age of ten, I received my first Holy Communion, and sixty years later remember the day clearly. Divine activity occurs–oftentimes giving us goosebumps and making us laugh. "She Who Shall Not Be Named," my procession partner, sat on my Communion candle, snapping it in half. As we processed out, everyone's candle was held upright, except mine, which drooped over at a right angle, making everyone laugh. When ritual takes on a life of its own, anything can happen.

What may appear to be less momentous occasions also call for ritual prayer. Appearances are not reality. Wanting a new job, beginning or ending a relationship, moving to a different place, all are soulful turning points calling us to do something prayerful in honor of the transition, something to help us get through. Endings and beginnings are always transformational turning points begging for divine intervention. Typically full of confusion, turning points often bear a call for ritual prayer. We need to be granted peace. When words feel empty and efforts not enough, souls call for the comforting power in ritual prayer to invite deities in for a spell. If the occasion is momentous, and you experience a need to respond in some soulful way, the call you hear may very well be inspired by ritual prayer–to drum up a little divine activity of your own. It all begins with the call. The fullest moment of grace, mystery, and magic is the call we hear to invite deities in for a spell and pray for a blessing.

HOLY ALTAR CALL

When we hear the call to pray, it's natural to feel a need to prepare a sacred place for divine intervention to occur. In thinking about home altars and folks making magic, there is nothing new under the sun. It's been going on since the beginning of time. Embedded deep within the soul of humanity is a longing to connect daily with who we know as God; a need for a room of our own, some place at home where no one will find or notice us. We need to unplug from the world, free ourselves from tensions that bind and distracting thoughts from the presence of others. The need to create sacred space is so deeply grounded in the soul that its origins far predate organized religion; it's what makes humanity divine. Souls long for solitude and a place for deities to abide.

Long before religion got organized, ancestors communed daily with their deities at home. In the beginning, altars were built in response to God who had just visited, marking the spot of divine intervention as holy. In every culture throughout history, home altars and images of deities are found. Sacred space was created in the home for deities to abide. All those I know who hear the call to pray also hear the call to create altars at home, to find a private corner where they can wrap themselves in solitude and commune with their God. Like our ancestors, we, too, feel the need to create sacred space at home, a divine door and threshold through which deities enter and stay for a spell, a holy place where we live and God abides with us.

My dearly departed mother, not church-going religious, but deeply spiritual in an ordinary way, built what I saw as an altar on top of a bookcase full of her favorite romance novels by Danielle Steel and Sandra Brown. I doubt she would have called it an altar, but it was covered with votive candles, statues of angels and saints–Mary and Jude her favorites–her mother's prayer book bulging with memorial cards of departed loved ones, rosaries, a crucifix, holy water, and a collection of religious artifacts from Indian missions asking for donations. Whenever someone needed help, she lit a candle. All lottery tickets leaned on Saint Jude, and photos of the great-grandkids stood around the angels. Over the years, more and more items appeared. When the great-grandkids brought her a rock, seashell, feather, or "penny from heaven" found on the sidewalk, it ended up on the altar. Postcards advertising the publication of my books and books of friends stood behind lit candles. Packs of matches from favorite restaurants collected in a small glass bowl, and my favorite, a musical Christmas angel snow globe, made in China, that plays "Beautiful Dreamer."

Every time I visited, more items had been added: an incense burner; box of frankincense; souvenirs from places she, friends, or family visited; and always a candle lit for some unspoken reason. By the time mom departed this life at the age of ninety, there wasn't an inch of space left on her bookcase of "spiritual reading." Her altar grew to be as richly full as her life.

In every religion, homes, temples, shrines, and churches build altars to mark the spot where divine intervention occurs, in much the same way we honor as sacred the places where something soulfully significant happened. It's not unusual to see white crosses along a country road or highway where someone departed this life in an accident, or mounds of flowers and burning votive candles at the scene of personal tragedy. In New York City, on 9/11, neighborhood streets were lined with posters of missing loved ones surrounded by flowers, candles, and heartfelt messages written on scraps of paper from passersby.

New York became a citywide altar in the weeks and months that followed. Downtown became transformed into holy ground as we breathed in what felt like soul dust for weeks. We mourned the loss of total strangers as we passed weeping loved ones on the street and offered sympathy. Ground Zero is memorialized forever as holy ground, an altar for everyone who visits to stand in the place where thousands departed this life at the same time, taking the city's breath away, a place of divine intervention. All over the world, places of disaster are also revered as holy ground. The door to the spirit world opened there, moving us to mark that spot as holy.

The manner of marking spots as holy can also be quite ordinary. Years ago, while walking to work, I noticed what looked like an art project in the trash at the curb, an icon of the Virgin Mary surrounded by red velvet, decorated with gold braiding and mounted on plywood. I removed it from the trash and stood it up against a nearby fence. If it was still there at the end of the day, I planned to make it mine. It *was* still there at the end of the day, but I didn't dare make it mine. Throughout the day, passersby transformed Curbside Trash Mary into a 43th Street shrine. Small bundles of fresh flowers–tulips, daisies, wilted roses–stood propped up on either side in wine-bottle vases, and three seven-day votive candles burned in front. Several pennies were scattered in front of the candles, as though wishes had been made, and a half-empty beer bottle, leading me to believe heart-felt prayers were offered there as well. Clearly, I wasn't the only one who stood in awe of the trash-day transformation. To this day, though decades later, I still cannot walk past that spot without hearing a call, though faint and small, to bow my head and remember. Even on the streets of New York City, and even on trash day, the holy altar call can be heard loud and clear by those who know how to see.

Whenever someone builds an altar–intentionally or coincidentally–it tends to be in response to something "holy" that happened there, perhaps a god who visited, a wish made, a prayer offered, even a romance novel loved, as though it was soulfully necessary to mark the spot as sacred, all of a sudden qualitatively different than any other space. The location appeared as a portal for divine intervention to occur; a door to the spirit world would open there with our prayer. Something extraordinary happened, some divinity appeared, making that spot holy, marking it as a place where deities visited and were likely to visit again. All of a sudden, ordinary space became enchanted, magic, sacred. All of a sudden, we're standing on holy ground. We build altars, enshrine them for protection, tend to them carefully with lit candles and fresh flowers, and return there when we hear the call to pray, when we feel a soulful need for divine intervention. Something or someone–the angel in our soul–moves us to respond naturally when extraordinary things happen–to mark spots on earth as holy, almost as a way of reminding all who pass by that we are not alone; deities abide with us.

All altars, including home altars, memorial grounds, cemeteries, and roadside shrines, are sites of great spiritual significance. They serve both as a door for deities to enter and intervene as well as a dwelling place for God to abide, so when we pass by we too can bow our head and remember. A soul departed this life on that spot, making it holy. Something extraordinary happened there, marking it as holy ground. Altars reveal how the holy is envisioned and present, the spot where divine activity occurs. Sacred places in the home appear on dresser tops, screened-in porches, window-sills, bookshelves, fireplace mantels, nightstands–any place we feel most inclined to welcome and receive divine company. The holy altar call is nothing more or less than finding a place where deities, angels, and saints can make themselves at home in our home; where all holy spirits, including our dearly departed loved ones, can stop by for a spell. The altar is a doorway to the spirit world that, when opened in ritual prayer, welcomes the presence of God, angels, and holy spirits. Holy. Holy. Holy.

Find Sacred Places

When it comes to finding sacred space in the home, follow gut instinct and you will be led to the perfect place. Along with millions of others, you may find the Chinese art of Feng Shui helpful in choosing a place and divining a space for your altar. Whatever place you choose, or whatever place chooses you, draws spiritual energy into your home. Finding the perfect place is the first step. Because most home altars develop spontaneously over time, you may already have found the most sacred spaces in your home and have begun to assemble objects holding special meaning and significance: photographs, seashells, statues, candles, rocks, incense, urns of dearly departed ashes, crystals, oils. No place or space in the home is inappropriate for an altar. Deities abide at home wherever we are.

The more frequently you feel called to ritual prayer, the more places you'll find divine activity occur. I have altars everywhere in my two-room New York City apartment. Over the years, slowly and surely, my apartment has become an altar. Bookshelf tops–housing all my favorite books of spiritual reading–have become places for "main altars"–bedroom altars where candles and incense are lit, prayers offered, and spells done. Covered with vintage hand-stitched linens found at flea markets, placed on one altar are statues of Buddha, Joan of Arc, my mother's statue of Saint Jude, two Mary shrines, votive candles, holy water and holy oils, photos of loved ones. On another main altar are ashes of my dearly departed, a Tibetan prayer bell, altar art made by friends, sacred stones from sacred sites–including Stonehenge–shells, an amethyst egg, a black marble egg, graveyard dirt from New Orleans ancestors, a Ouija board, a magic wand made by a Wiccan priest friend, rosaries, beads and medals of saints, a box of feathers found, and my mother's musical Christmas angel snow globe that plays "Beautiful Dreamer." My life's treasures live on the altar.

In the living room, on top of the west wall bookcase, facing east, is a thirty-year collection of statues and religious artifacts, each of its shelves lined with old family photos, nun figurines, friends' artwork, vintage artifacts and toys–all treasures kept for lifetimes. Walls are covered with art, most paintings by friends, a hand-stitched *Mano Poderosa*, and religious art "rescued" from flea markets. Even kitchen and bathroom walls are covered with art, every room with candles to burn, a reminder for all who enter of the deities, angels, and saints who abide with me. Psychic friends who stay in my apartment when I travel remind me of the "spirit activity" in these two rooms of my own; all of it hospitable. That's what altars do in the home–reveal how sacred the space is where we live. There is no place more sacred and more soulful than where we wake up, where we sleep, where we love, where we laugh and cry, where we celebrate, where we rest at the end of the day and enjoy the pleasure of company or solitary splendor. Homes are the most natural places for altars because that's where we abide, and that's where deities and holy spirits abide with us.

Some find entranceways in the home divine places for an altar, believing everyone who enters is an angel in disguise. *"Don't be afraid to have strangers in your house, for some have entertained angels unknowingly."* (Hebrews 13:2) Most religious traditions, such as Judaism, Catholicism, and Buddhism, have rituals for entering and leaving the home. For example, it's an old, nearly gone custom among Catholics to bless themselves with holy water and a Sign of the Cross. Holy water fonts were hung on the wall near the front and back door. My Jewish neighbors kiss their fingertips before rubbing the mezuzah in the doorway for a blessing. Buddhists remove their shoes, believing that, in entering your home, they stand on holy ground. In the entranceway to my apartment is a cast-iron votive stand from a local church sale. When calls come with requests for prayers, candles are lit for their intention. Visitors, and the little ones I tutor, light candles and make wishes there. Possibly for hundreds of years candles have been lit on that votive stand, believing as I do, making it an extra powerful place for prayers to be answered favorably and wishes granted. Doorway blessings are some of the most ancient rituals we know, marking entranceways as perfect spots for altars and shrines, blessing all who come and go, including yourself.

Many also find, as I do, that bedrooms are naturally perfect places for altars. Deities and angels have a reputation for visiting in sleep and dreams, and bedroom altars open the door into the spirit world nightly. Bedroom altars provide the uniqueness of solitude and privacy, not easily found in dining rooms, living rooms, and entrance ways. We tend to wind down in the bedroom, begin and end our day, shift gears and read, make love, calm the soul in preparing to sleep. Exclusive privacy and protection essential for personal and ritual prayer are easily available in bedrooms. Facing the altar at the beginning and end of every day also energizes the spirit within us and our home. Being surrounded by sacred stuff makes us feel better. We absorb the energy. Our spirit is lifted up in wakening and carried through the day, as well as granted peace at night in preparing to sleep. Bedroom altars offer the best conditions for divine activity.

Over the years, you too may be likely to find, as I have, several altars in your home, and if you have front and back yards, outdoor shrines too. I have two main multipurpose altars, and several side altars dedicated to specific purposes: one honoring dearly departed loved ones, a mermaid shrine in the bathroom, a side altar for babies (new souls entering or having departed this world), a votive stand for the wishes of those who visit, and a doorway shrine to bless all comings and goings. All appeared over time, as spirit moved, and all were created to mark and honor the place where divine activity occurs. I suspect once you find sacred space to create your altar, you too will find, over time, altars everywhere. It may start with a candle, flowers, then photos, artifacts, stones, and shells. Follow your spirit in discerning sacred places and you too may gradually find yourself surrounded by altars.

Create Sacred Space

Once you've found a sacred place for your altar, the next step is creating sacred space. In creating sacred spaces, I find it helpful to consider placement of the altar, purifying or cleansing the space, and assembling sacred objects. It's the fine mix of all three–the Holy Trinity of altars–which transforms ordinary places into sacred spaces. By the power of those three, homes become dwelling places for deities and holy spirits. Having altars everywhere is enough to make me feel better day by day, nearly indestructible at times. Being surrounded by sacred objects, charged as they are with divine energy that grows with every prayer offered and candle lit, endows us naturally with a sense of comfort and well-being. Without a doubt, you too will find in creating sacred space, divine sources of strength and fountains of peace. Home altars remind us constantly we are not alone. Deities abide within.

In considering placement of the altar, you may find it helpful to consider the direction you want to face: east, west, north, or south. Associated with the rising sun, east is the place of new beginnings and new life. If your life is aching for breakthroughs, and your soul is longing for new life, you may want to place your altar facing east. One of my main altars faces east. The south is often seen as the place of growth and expansion, so if you feel your life needs wider, more open spaces, then facing your altar toward the south may be most helpful. The west, land of the setting sun, is the direction to face when transformation and change are needed in your life. And facing north, as my main altar does now, puts us in the direction of the soul and the deepest, most mysterious dimensions of life. Whatever direction you align yourself with for the placement of your altar serves to draw divine energy into your life and your home. In creating space for the placement of your altar, therefore, consider soulfully the direction toward which your life is drawn. Given different needs at different times in life, you may develop, as I have, altars facing all four directions: the Buddha altar faces north, the Mary altar faces east, the votive stand in the entranceway faces west, and the ancestor altar faces south. I find great comfort in having all bases covered.

The next step in creating sacred space is purifying and cleansing the altar. In the Catholic ritual of Eucharist—Mass and Communion—just before the time of consecration when bread and wine become divine, the altar is prepared and purified with incense and holy water. The priest adds frankincense and myrrh to burning coals and proceeds to incense the four corners of the altar, above, below, and all around. He then incenses the servers on the altar, who in turn incense the congregation and the priest as well, all in preparation for divine intervention. The same ritual is repeated with holy water, sometimes too vigorously. Those who either sat in the front pew or at the end of the pew often got saturated with holy water by an overzealous priest or altar boy—always a bit of comic relief at a high holy moment, leading me to believe deities possess a finely tuned sense of humor.

In cleansing and purifying altar space, I encourage you to do the same with incense or smudge stick (bundles of dried sage). Any incense can be used, and smudge sticks can either be home-made or purchased easily. Light the end of bundled dried sage, or incense stick, and pass the smoke over, under, and around the space, as well as around the room in which the altar is placed. Do the same with holy water. Sprinkle on top of the altar, along the sides, and underneath. Also sprinkle holy water around the room, especially in the corners. Whatever you find most natural and helpful is best. I use incense and holy water, not only to purify altar space, but also to completely clear the mind and prepare the soul–the inner altar–for divine intervention. If you're allergic to smoke, holy water purifies and blesses just as well. Holy water can be found in any Catholic Church, or you can do the "Full Moon Holy Water Blessing" (p. 122) and make your own. We all have the soulful "priestly" power to bring out the holiness in water.

Once you've found the place and prepared the space, you can begin the spiritual process of assembling sacred objects to be placed on your altar. What makes objects sacred? The energy from what happens around them and how much we love them. When objects become saturated with the energy of what we love, they become holy. Objects loved and treasured, passed down from generations of loved ones–particularly jewelry–naturally become sacred over time; so much so we take every measure to ensure our favorite things are passed on and cared for long after we're gone. The longer objects are loved, cared for, and revered, the more sacred they become, bearing the love of all who owned them. It is most fitting then for most sacred objects to be kept on your altar. Nothing is inappropriate for your altar if it holds meaning for you, and nothing is profane for those who know how to see.

Religious objects and images, having been worshipped and prayed over for centuries—some thousands of years—become most sacred, making them most fit to be placed on an altar. In the center of my main altar stands a nineteenth-century wood carved Virgin Mary from the Philippines, found in an antique shop. She has no hands, and facial features are worn smooth. Half the moon under her feet is gone, but the face of the angel holding up the other half is still there. The divine energy of being prayed to and loved for centuries is also still there. I heard her speak. It's not unusual to be moved by ancient religious art or images. Look at any statue of Buddha and you're granted peace instantly. My mother's statue of Saint Jude is charged with her prayerful energy and his. Certain works of art naturally "speak" to us, and that kind of speaking is full of what makes objects holy. Because some images represent visions of the sacred, it's natural to be moved by them to pray, lifting us from wherever we are to soulful places of comfort and peace. All works of art, I believe, represent moments of inspiration, creation, divine intervention—they belong on an altar.

Visit the Metropolitan Museum of Art in New York City. Find the paintings of Joan of Arc and Mary Magdalene, sit there for a while, and see for yourself how naturally souls are moved by art and how divine the experience feels–out of body, out of this world. They speak to you. Van Gogh felt the same. *"When I have a terrible need of–shall I say the word–religion–then I go out and paint the stars."* Visit New York City's MOMA (Museum of Modern Art) and stand before Van Gogh's "Starry Night"–close enough to reach out and touch–the essence of, shall I say the word, religion. All works of art are expressions of divine intervention, capable of revealing glimpses of the deities. Any work of art you love speaks in ways other works don't. Images that speak, hold your attention, and move your soul belong on your altar. They bear the divine energy of their creator, becoming a portal for the voices of deities to speak.

Objects representing the divine power in nature–earth, air, fire, water–also belong on an altar. Those who see this world charged with the grandeur of God do not find it hard to believe all elements of Creation are alive in mysterious ways. Everything has a soul. Everything in heaven and on earth, everything in Creation, bears the "name of the Lord" and begs to be honored as such–never taken in vain. Rocks and earth from Stonehenge, Jerusalem, and the Holy Land or any sacred site naturally feel sacred to believers and nonbelievers alike, in ways rocks and dirt from a shopping mall parking lot might not. In the good old days, stones were worshipped as living embodiments of divine life, making them even more worthy to be kept on an altar. Native Americans believe mountains are the homes of the deities, and anyone who's been up close and personal with a mountain wouldn't dare disagree. Primitive altars were made of stone. Walk through any flea market or antique store and you may find, as I always do, objects that "speak," objects bearing the energy of previous owners. Vibes are good or bad. Because of the surrounding energy, ordinary objects become qualitatively charged, become treasure or trash. Objects that speak and move us with meaning become sacred; they too belong on the altar.

In the Catholic tradition, relics from saints were often miniscule pieces of cloth that touched the bones or the burial place of one revered as holy. All of a sudden, just with a touch, ordinary cloth becomes sacred. I suspect we all share a desire to own a little piece of those we love, so much so even the smallest, most ordinary inanimate objects become alive, become sacred. Bracelets my mother wore every day, I wear every day, keeping connected in spirit. In revering something as sacred, objects become something else, something holy, even though physical appearance remains the same. Appearances are not reality. The most ordinary objects become treasure, become holy, when charged with the energy of loved ones. Everything is intrinsically holy for those who know how to see all of nature revealing the sacred. Nothing is inappropriate for the altar. Personal treasures, religious items, and objects from nature all belong on our altar.

My life is on the main altar, covered with hand-embroidered linens from the flea market; statues of Mary from Mexico, Peru, and the Philippines; and statues of Buddha, Saint Dymphna, and Joan of Arc. Seven votive candles burn every day, surrounded by rocks from Stonehenge, Easter Island, and other sacred sites. Scattered nearby are crystals, holy water, anointing oils, incense, a ceramic container with dirt from the New Orleans grave of my grandmother and godmother, little urns of ashes from my mother, Shirley, and best friend, Molly, and the treasured rosary from Sister Concilio, the ninety-four-year-old nun who helped me survive my first five years in the convent. In assembling objects for your altar, I encourage you to do the same. Put your life on the altar, surrounding it with naturally divine elements of earth, air, fire, and water. The altar is you and what you find most holy. Let intuition–the angel in your soul– your holy spirit–be your guide. Once sacred space is created in your home, you will find the call to ritual prayer and divine activity become more frequent, more a part of everyday life. Before you know it, and almost without notice, the call to engage in the magic of ritual prayer will become your daily bread–the most divine way to begin, get through, and end every day. Blessed be. Blessed be. Blessed be.

*The most incredible thing about miracles
is that they happen.*

– G. K. CHESTERTON

MAGIC OF RITUAL

The magic of ritual, like the call to pray, is and is not as mysterious as it sounds. When something we want to happen becomes real, that's magic. Something we envision becomes true. The invisible is made visible. Yet getting what we want oftentimes doesn't seem to be nearly as mysterious as how it happened, how we got what we prayed for, how the magic in ritual works. We know what it looks like. Through a friend of a friend, a stranger, or some coincidence, a prayer is answered. Obstacles are removed and our wish is granted. Closed doors open and opportunities appear. That's the point at which we look back, scratch our heads, and wonder *"How did that happen?"* What elements came together to answer our prayer? What ingredients make the magic in ritual work? How do we create magically favorable moments? In the deep, dark, unseen world of miraculous events, it doesn't get more mysterious. Making the invisible visible is the most magic work of all. We knock and the door opens, we seek and find what we're looking for, we ask and our wish is granted. That is the divine power in ritual. We folks make magic.

Einstein believed the most beautiful thing humans can experience is the mysterious. And even though what we want may not become real immediately, or as soon as we wish, something happens every time we pray. That's mysterious. Medical science also recognizes as true the amazing and mysterious power of prayer, once, twice, even three times removed. Praying for ourselves, our loved ones, even those we don't know at all, somehow works. What we pray for happens. The woman who couldn't get pregnant after multiple failed attempts conceives and brings healthy and happy babies into this world. The clinically depressed feel better. An incurable disease stops progressing, even though there is no cure. That's no big insight on my part or that of medical science. In Christian scripture, Christ reveals if we do not hesitate in our heart, if there is no doubt at all, if we believe what we say, it will be granted. It's that simple. *"Whatever you ask for prayerfully, believe that you will receive, and it will come to you."* (Mark 11:23-24). Saint Augustine found, *"Faith is to believe what we do not see. The reward of this faith is to see what we believe."* There is divine power in faith. We get what we ask for. We see what we believe. Dreams become true. Abracadabra.

Questions always linger over why bad things happen to good people. Why don't we always get what we pray for? Because, as the priestly Teilhard de Chardin believed, *"We are not human beings on a spiritual journey. We are spiritual beings on a human journey."* We are spirits experiencing what it means to be human. Bad things happen to everyone because suffering is a big part of what it means to be human. That's life. Bad stuff happens. Everything comes with a purpose, a message, a lesson to be learned. All the money in the world can't pay for a life without suffering. Pain, suffering, sickness, death, tragedy, disappointment, loss–all happen to good and bad alike because it's part of the human journey, part of the mystery of our lives. No one enters or departs this life without the experience of suffering. While we may sometimes feel as though we get more than our fair share, Socrates suggests, *"If all our misfortunes were laid in one common heap whence everyone must take an equal portion, most people would be content to take their own and depart."* Our mission in this lifetime is to live through the sorrowful mysteries of our life with the same soulful acceptance and peace we feel with joyful mysteries, with "evenness of mind." We are called to find heaven in all the hell on earth.

What is it about suffering that makes it essential to the human experience? Why can't we live without it? What makes suffering so essential to the human experience is the miraculous way in which it changes us instantly. The most sorrowful mysteries of our lives are also the most powerful. Nothing wakes us up and changes us more quickly or completely than suffering–especially sickness, death, loss–full of transformational powers so divine that Christian scripture reveals it can even raise new life from the dead. Something awful happens, and our lives come to a screeching halt. We don't know what hit us. We feel paralyzed with grief, pain, and sorrow, so much so the hardest part of the day is waking up and barely having the energy to get out of bed. Any experience full of devastating power to tear our life apart is also full of divine power to pull us back together, if we let it. Between suffering striking and our response, there is a space, a magically favored space where anything can happen. In that holy space lies the power to make miracles. The miracle lies in what we do when bad things happen; how we respond when awful events upend our life; how we get through the worst of times in the best possible way. This is the sacred space where the magic in prayer does its most powerful work. This is when we are given the opportunity to let the transformational power in suffering raise us from the dead. What we do with what happens makes all the difference in our world, if we let it. Letting it be is a secret power waiting to be found in all suffering. Everything is holy just the way it is.

Understanding what happens when we pray is the ultimate mystery because it calls us to see the unseen; changes the way we see. In prayer, we begin to look beyond appearances into the heart of the matter where life changes. Appearances are not reality. Beneath the surface of events that tend to toss us back and forth with miserable feelings lies the heart of the matter bearing lessons to be learned, truths to be revealed, peace and comfort to be granted. Divine activity occurs in prayer, moving us in ways we may not see or feel instantly and certainly don't understand. Even so, transformation occurs. Something happens, like scenery changes in the dark during acts in a play. We cannot sit for a spell with deities and walk away untouched, even though we may feel that way at first. We are asked not to grieve endlessly because what we have lost will return to us in another form. Hidden within the worst of times are the best of times to come.

Blank empty times when we feel stuck with nothing happening, feeling neither here nor there, are what mystics call "clouds of unknowing" and "dark nights of the soul." Something's happening, but we are completely in the dark not knowing what it is, so much so it feels nothing is happening at all–*nada, nada, nada*–except fearing and doubting what we want will ever become real. We'd even bet our bottom dollar the sun will not come out tomorrow. As the anonymous author of the *Cloud of Unknowing* reveals, we feel "suspended in mid-air with nothing to lean on." Times of unknowing are mysteries in all our lives. That's also when the magic in prayer does its most effective work because we do not have energy to interfere or resist. When we feel dead inside, lifeless, not knowing what to do, where to go, what to think or how to feel, magic is happening. Something is brewing, something is stirring, something is asking us to be still and know all shall be well. Miracles brew most powerfully in the darkest nights of our souls.

Not all reality is physical—we are never as dead as we feel—and not all magic manifests in ways we immediately see or understand. Again, appearances are not reality. What we see happening is the tip of what's really going on in the depths of the soul, which we can't see clearly. The world we're talking about here is spiritual, having to do with the inner life, the life of the soul, where outcomes cannot be forced or controlled, no matter how good the intention. That's not how holy spirits work. This is the world of the soul, Innerland, where we're initially clueless about how things work. Because rituals and spells draw us into the spirit world, their magic works in soul time, spirit time, where hours, days, weeks, and years mean nothing. The wheels of divine activity grind exceedingly slow and exceedingly fine, all the while revealing everything is holy just as it is. Everything—the best of times and the worst of times—comes with a purpose, lessons to learn for wishes to be granted. Everything that happens calls us to perform the prayerful magic of being our best self, even when we could not possibly feel worse. Whenever we experience change—no matter how disruptive—we can be sure our life is being worked on by deities; we are being made better. What is happening in our life always belongs on the altar.

Whenever we pray, whenever we engage in rituals, we enter into sacred space wherein deities dwell and anything can happen, the divine world of magic wherein what we need most will be given.

Erasmus assures us, *"Bidden or unbidden, God is present,"* but it's we who tend to be nowhere nearly as present. It's hard to sit still and be present during the worst of times, fearing awful feelings will only intensify making us feel worse. Escaping feels better as does numbing the pain, until we discover we only feel more awful, more depressed, more stuck. In trying to sit still, minds wander, and we follow disturbing thoughts, jump into any distraction we think of, and don't want to sit still. Even so, making ourselves sit still, even for ten minutes, allows the presence of God to stir things up in the depths of the soul, beyond the busyness of our thoughts and the weakness of our will, granting us some measure of peace and comfort, freeing us to feel noticeably better. G. K. Chesterton agrees: *"In the struggle for existence, it is only on those who hang on for ten minutes after all is hopeless, that hope begins to dawn."* Something happens every time we pray, working the kind of magic that transforms awful feelings into feeling better. In the depths of the soul, our life is changed every time we pray, every time we sit still for a spell.

What happens in the presence of God has everything to do with becoming more capable of living differently–kinder, more generous and accepting, braver, less angry, less judgmental, even funnier. Though we may feel nothing is happening, as though we're talking to ourselves and wasting time, nothing can be further from truth. We are being moved profoundly in ways we may not feel instantly or understand. Everything that happens calls us to become better not worse, urging greater acceptance and inclusiveness, honoring the presence of God in all Creation, seeing in every face, in every living being the image of God. That's the mystery in ritual prayer and therein lies its magic; in everything that happens we are called to let God be love in us. Something life-changing happens every time we open the door to the spirit world in prayer, enter into sacred space for a visit with deities, even if we don't feel the immediate gratification of seeing or understanding what it is. Always bow in gratitude for whatever happened in prayer in preparation for being granted what you need most. Or, as Native American wisdom reveals, *"Give thanks for unknown blessings already on their way."*

Because the magic of ritual lies in the spiritual world of being transformed by mysterious activity—something really does happen—an attempt is made here to understand what elements converge in ritual to make magic. How do we create moments favorable for magic to happen? For every moment that's magical, for every movement that grants wishes, there appears to be the right time, the right mix of ingredients, and the right constellation of elements to generate divine activity. When all cylinders in life click into place, magic happens. I found four ingredients, when mixed together, tend to make the magic in ritual work most effectively: the power in *belief*, the power in *necessity*, the power in *nature*, and the power in *repetition*. All four reveal why, when, where, and how ritual prayer works, and all four, when synchronized, put us in touch with the divine power in ritual, showing us how to make magic.

Belief

Everything I know and believe about the power in prayer and the magic in ritual comes from what I was told as a child about Santa Claus and what I found true as an adult in Christian scripture: If you don't believe, you don't receive. Thoughts, desires, wishes, and prayers are powerful tools in the life of the spirit, and what makes magic work more than anything else is the divine power in faith. Believing is the source and center of all spiritual life, the air holy spirits breathe, the stuff of divine intervention. We are what we believe. If we believe all are created in the image and likeness of God, we naturally love another as we long to be loved and make peace on earth. If we do not believe all are created equal, we inevitably become racist, sexist, and exclusive with hate-filled hearts, making hell on earth for all those not created in our image and likeness. That's how powerful thoughts are. We are what we think.

If in prayer we believe what we say will happen, with no doubt in our heart, what we ask for will be granted. Christian scripture reveals, *"Let it be as you believe."* (Matthew 9:29)

Everyone who has a miracle is told by Christ it's because of their faith that miracles happened. Faith sees life differently. The eyes of faith see with soul, looking beyond attention-grabbing appearances into what's going on, what's happening that we can't see. For most, it takes time to see clearly what's going on. Rarely do we feel instantly better in ways we want, making belief harder. Learning to see with the eyes of the soul takes time, divine time, begging us to persevere, to continue believing without a doubt that what we ask for in prayer will come at the perfect time, already on its way. Only by the divine power in faith do closed doors open when we knock, reveal what we're looking for, grant whatever we wish. We may even receive far more than we ask for or imagine—mountains may be moved—such is divine power in faith. The most important ritual element in making magic is the divine power of belief.

Hesitation is the greatest obstacle to faith capable of moving mountains, and lingering doubt slowly drains all hope from dreams. While pure belief may appear naive, childish, foolish, nothing more than wishful thinking, it also has everything to do with releasing miraculous powers in prayer and ritual. Hesitation or doubt is all it takes to break the spell. If we doubt the divine power in faith by focusing on what's not happening, nothing will change in our favor and we are likely to feel worse, hopeless. We have no ability to see beyond appearances, nor can we understand the purpose behind events or life lessons intended for us to learn. In order to make magic in ritual prayer, we must summon within us the divine power in faith, which opens the door to the spirit world and welcomes divine intervention. We must believe we shall receive what we wish and pray for without question, giving no thought to when, where, and how our prayer will be answered.

Divine power in belief is released most powerfully when we leave details to the deities. So great is divine power in faith that mountains can not only be moved, but can be lifted up and hurled into the sea. A Chinese proverb also reveals mountains will move "when sleeping women wake." That's how quickly and effectively, more than we can ask for or imagine, the greatest obstacles in life can be moved by the waking power in prayer. In prayer we are wakened into a world where miracles happen. The most important ingredient in releasing the magic in ritual is the divine power in faith. Believing we've already received what we asked for jump-starts and charges the magic in ritual. Faith is the heart and soul of all magic. It's the divine power in belief that fills life with magically favored moments, experiences of heaven on earth.

Belief's soulmate in the magic of ritual is focus, focus, focus. Focus is singlehearted concentration on one thing, excluding attention to anything other than what we ask for in prayer.

The divine power in belief is intensified by the ability to focus attention in one direction. Be very specific in focusing your request, aiming the power of your faith on harming no one, and letting only goodness, kindness, and compassion work through you. The reason for focusing the power of prayer on what is good, right, just, and holy has everything to do with the law of Karma: whatever you put out there will come back to you, not only in kind, but ten times over. It has everything to do with every true religion's Golden Rule: do unto others as you want others to do to you, because what you do to others will indeed be done to you in time, for better or worse. It's a divine law of nature. So be very careful with wishes. Never ask something for yourself at the expense of someone else. Ask instead for all obstacles to be removed, clearing the way for your prayer to be answered. The most important ingredient in focusing the power of our prayer is always love sweet love. The love in our heart and the faith in our soul spark the magic in ritual to grant what we ask, bringing out how divine we humans can be.

Perseverance is the soul-saving element that intensifies the divine power in belief, preventing us from giving up, abandoning hope, and losing faith. In prayer, we are given the grace, energy, and insight to persevere, if we have the eyes of faith to see. Only those who never give up learn to see in the dark. How can we persevere when it feels as though nothing's happening? Gravitate toward what feels better. Choose to do what makes you happy, surround yourself with friends who are fun to be with, harmonize with whatever brings you freedom, growth, and joy. You can choose the thought that makes you worry or the thought that makes you happy. You have that choice in every moment. In your perseverance, therefore, choose to feel happy anyhow. Reach for a thought that feels better. Count your blessings. Focus on the goodness in your life, and the door to the spirit world will remain open by the power in your faith, granting you peace while the magic in what you ask for becomes manifest. Confidence and faithfulness are required to persevere through the worst of times. Confidence that what we ask for will be granted, and faithfulness in never giving up. Perseverance is the air faith breathes while we wait, keeping faith alive, charging it with divine energy to make magic.

*If one advances confidently in the
direction of his dreams, and endeavors
to live the life which he has imagined, he
will meet with a success unexpected
in common hours.*

–Henry David Thoreau

Necessity

When it comes to focusing the power in prayer, we only need to look at our life. Pressure points, sore spots, places of greatest tension–all hold the divine power in necessity. There is a sense of soulful urgency in times of necessity, those times when we cry out for mercy, cling to hope, the point of pleading and begging when we cry out with the Psalmist *"How long, O God, how long?"* The more urgent and intense the need, the more highly charged it is with divine energy. Even though all we may feel is hell on earth, inner tensions are signs of divine activity breaking through, full of grace to transform us into our best self. Whatever feels most urgent, most necessary, most beyond our control, begs to be put on the altar. The intensity of energy embedded in necessity fuels the making of magic, the summoning of divine intervention, the breeding of miracles. Exploding points release torrents of energy, soulful anguish leaves us speechless, depression intensifies darkness, all generating the kind of necessity essential to making magic in ritual prayer. Everything is holy just as it is. Everything in our life is the stuff of which miracles are made, most especially the painful stuff charged with the divine power of necessity.

Deities have a long-standing reputation for appearing in storms, even causing them. Some are known to throw lightning bolts in order to wake us up. In ancient myths, texts, and scriptures, our ancestors tell stories of creator and destroyer deities who governed the mysteries of life. The human experience is full of joyful and sorrowful mysteries. And it's the divine activity of the destroyer deities who whip up storms in our lives and plunge us into life's most sorrowful mysteries, leaving us in the depths of an abyss full of darkness. Times of greatest necessity are given as divine opportunities for growth and insight. As the Sufi mystic Rumi advises, *"Do not worry that your life is turning upside down. How do you know that the side you are used to is better than the one to come?"* While tensions and anxieties may feel more disturbing than divine at first, they're revealed as a divine sign for those who believe, marking the spot of dire necessity, the sacred place to focus our attention and God's. The starting point for all ritual prayer is always the point of greatest necessity.

Whatever urgent needs we know, therein lies the divine power of necessity and its ability to transform the way we feel. Necessity is not only the mother of invention, it's also the creator of magic, the mother of divine intervention. Deities only want what's in hearts and souls. The most important stuff in our life becomes the divine stuff of magic and miracles. What we need most attracts the attention of God. In focusing prayerfully on the mysteries of our lives, we welcome divine intervention in a way nothing else can. That's how extraordinarily powerful the necessities of life are in making magic. It can't happen without us and the most important stuff of our lives. Whether it be the pain and sadness of loss, the bewilderment of confusion, or the pure joy of dreams come true, the magic in prayer always comes from the sorrowful and joyful mysteries of our life, always has to do with the inner necessity in our heart's most urgent desire. Never underestimate the power of magic hidden in necessity.

In focusing the power of belief and necessity in prayer, begin with what's happening in your life. Wherever the happy and sad places are, so too are the makings of magic. Moments of bewilderment, bad news, tensions, good news, and pain put us in touch with the deepest mysteries of life. The way life unfolds rarely coincides perfectly with our expectations, and whenever upsets happen, we can be sure divine activity is at work. Bad news and misery are mysterious facts of life that always throw us into a state where we naturally cry out of the depths for help, naturally feel the need for divine intervention. Focus the power of necessity on any mystery in your life, put that divine stuff on the altar, let the magic in prayer do its work, and believe your wish is granted. Prayers are answered in the asking, knocking is the key in opening doors, and in seeking we've already found what we're looking for.

The divine power hidden in necessity calls us to trust the divine power hidden in waiting. Most moments of necessity rise from something for which we've been waiting a long time, dreams we've been waiting a lifetime to come true, the growing intensity present within the need for something to happen. What we do while we wait makes all the difference in our life. Waiting is a time of transition and transformation in which we are called to let it be. This is the time when what was lost leads to find something new, where ends turn into new beginnings, when the darkest night shows us how to see in the dark, when what feels dead in us rises and shines in new life. In many ways, these times feel like days in the tomb between death and resurrection when the divine power in necessity is operating at its fullest, bringing life out of death, light out of darkness, everlasting happiness out of soulful sadness. In times of greatest necessity, while we wait for miracles to manifest, what we do is critical to what happens next.

What do we do while we wait that makes all the difference in our life? During this holiest of time between here and there, between death and resurrection, ends and new beginnings, we are called upon to "brood" over miracles in the making. In the earliest myths of Creation, the Deity broods over the Cosmic Egg until new life breaks through and Creation is born. This kind of brooding is the divine opposite of sulking, the kind of brooding we know all too well how to do. This is the brooding of the chicken on the egg. We can only imagine what the chicken is thinking, or if she is thinking at all. I suspect she sits there contemplatively, doing nothing but keeping the egg warm and letting it be, envisioning her chicks waiting to be born. This is the kind of brooding we're called to do in times of greatest necessity. In ritual prayer, we are called to lay our eggs of greatest need on the altar and let it be. At most, we are called to do nothing but focus on the happiest of thoughts, envisioning what life will be like when our dream comes true, how happy we will be when the miracle we pray for happens.

What happens while we wait, while we sit upon a heap of doing nothing, is a kind of transformation we hardly notice at first. While we wait prayerfully, we are given grace–insight–enabling us to see more clearly what we couldn't see before. We learn to see in the dark. We begin to understand what before was beyond our understanding, incomprehensible. Next steps appear, blowing wind beneath our wings, enabling us to move forward. Paralyzing misery may be lifted, allowing us to feel better, even leading to growing moments of happiness. We may begin to know how surrounded we are by angels and spirit guides sent to help, comfort, lead in the direction of new life. We see most clearly all the ways in which we are not alone. In ritual prayer, we summoned deities and prayed for divine intervention. While we wait in dire necessity, brooding and not sulking, our prayer is answered. We are granted divine assistance to help through our darkest days, leading forward into the brightest light of new life. While we wait, we are transformed in soulful ways, planting our feet firmly on the path to becoming our best, most divine self. We become experts at finding heaven in all the hell on earth.

Whatever it is about the mysterious workings of faith and necessity, one thing we know for sure: their power to summon deities is both extraordinary and transformational. Whenever we feel inner tension, whenever we experience dire inner necessity, there it is that the divine work of transformation has begun. All those icky feelings are signs of life being changed. That's what transformation feels like in the beginning. That's how we know our prayer is being heard. That's when we notice the need for something to change, for something to happen, for some kind of divine intervention to alter positively the way we feel and the course of our life. Endings always bear starting points for some kind of new life, full of miraculous energy known to raise life from what feels so dead. That's where ritual prayer does its best work in changing hearts, minds, and souls in ways nothing else can. That is magic, pure and simple. That is the point at which we begin to see clearly what T. S. Eliot saw, *"I had seen birth and death but had thought they were different."* Abracadabra.

Nature

Aligning ourselves with the divine powers in heaven and on earth is the third element in making magic through ritual prayer. The world is charged with divine energy, stamped with the image and likeness of God, whose name "Yahweh" means "One who brings to be." All of nature–the heavens and the earth–are given to help "bring to be" what we ask for in prayer, so much so we can see the seasons of our lives mirrored in the seasons of nature. I suspect we all know times that feel like spring, full of new life; summer when we wallow in warmth and well-being; fall when things begin to change and loss is felt; and winter when darkness grows and we feel the need to hibernate. In preparing ritual prayer, therefore, spend time thinking about where in nature you see your life unfolding. The primitive belief in the synchronicity of nature and religious rituals reveals divine power at its highest when we align ourselves with the cycles of nature, when we tune into the movements of heaven and earth with our prayer. The seasons of the year, the cycles of the moon, and the movement of the planets bear divine energy to increase significantly the power in our prayers and rituals. As above, so below.

Because everything on earth is charged with the presence of God–rocks, water, fire, crystals, flowers, trees, herbs, plants– bringing those elements into our ritual prayer intensifies the power in making magic. Some of the most powerful rituals I've known have taken place on the shores of Lake Michigan under a full moon, or at sunrise and sunset, and in the forest-like backyard of a friend under a full harvest moon. Indoor rituals around the dining room table, surrounded by flowers, fruits and vegetables from the garden, candlelight, wine, and the company of loved ones become equally divine. In preparing ritual prayer, call on the power present in all the gifts of the earth, even the presence of pets and animals whose souls are pure and their ability to see into the spirit world finely tuned. The more inclusive you are in bringing the divine power of the earth into your rituals, the more highly charged the ritual becomes in making magic. The holy spirits present in the earth are with you.

Because everything in the heavens is also charged with the divine energy, aligning yourself with the phases of the moon, movements of the planets, equinoxes, and eclipses intensifies the power in your ritual to make magic. Consult astrologers in choosing the perfect date and time for your ritual or, as I have done, begin collecting books on astrology and learning how to synchronize your rituals with heavenly powers. Calling on the presence of angels, saints, and spirit guides in your ritual–all divine heavenly powers–brings a highly charged presence into your prayer, as well as into your life. Dearly departed loved ones lend the same divine intervention when called upon, eager to help answer your prayer, remaining with you wherever you are. Acknowledging the presence of spirits and calling on their divine energy for help further intensify the making of magic. Repeatedly calling on all heavenly powers in ritual prayer will strengthen you in knowing heavenly holy spirits are with you.

Our earliest ancestors believed prayers and rituals were necessary to turn the seasons of the year; to help transform summer into fall, fall into winter, winter into spring, and spring into summer; such is the power of nature in ritual prayer. They believed the divine power in prayer kept time moving. Since the beginning of time, the power in the changing seasons of nature has always been a divine ingredient in creating magic in ritual. It is no accident or coincidence therefore that Christians celebrate Christmas and Jews celebrate Hanukkah at the time of the winter solstice, the longest night and shortest day of the year. It's the "O Holy Night" wherein light overcomes the dark and the season of increasing daylight begins. We celebrate the birth of light on the darkest night of the year. Associated in nature with the birth of the Sun, the holiest of days was designated by early Christianity as the birthday of Christ–Son of God and Light of the World–bringing their God in line with all the Sun deities of mythology born on the night of the winter solstice. O Holy Night indeed. In a similar manner, Easter, the highest holy day on the Christian calendar, celebrates the death and resurrection of Christ at the time of the spring equinox, when new life is resurrected every year from the dead cold of winter into the warm rebirth of spring when all of nature comes to life again. In the spring, Passover also celebrates freedom from the darkness of slavery into the divine life of freedom. I also believe *There is no such thing as coincidence,* and nothing could be truer to that belief than organized religion's synchronistic timing of its holiest days with nature's most powerful turning points.

In planning spells and rituals, magic power is intensified in paying attention to the seasons of the year, the phases of the moon, and the movement of planets. Similarly, gathering together elements of the earth in preparing ritual prayer further intensifies divine energy in making magic. Align the mysteries in your life with the transformations in heaven and earth, and see how highly charged those moments become. The Greek word *Kairos* captures the essence of those moments as "magically favored." The divine power in nature reveals death is never final, always followed closely by some manifestation of new life, revealing divine cycles in all life. Even when we feel devastated by loss and death, the divine power in nature reveals new life embedded in the darkest days; new life will appear in the deadest of times. In the spirit world, endings are full of magic in creating new beginnings, and souls bear the divine power of the phoenix, rising from ashes over and over, into the fullness of life. Aligning ourselves with the divine transformations in heaven and on earth provides a powerful charge to the magic in ritual. Heaven and earth join in answering your prayer.

Repetition

Repetition is the secret of probability, according to Carl Jung, meaning the more we repeat certain activities, the greater the chance of getting a desired outcome. The more we repeat prayers and rituals, the better and more comfortable we become. We become more powerful in a way, more effective in manifesting what we want. Practice makes perfect. Meaning also intensifies when rituals are repeated, which is to say, the more we repeat rituals, the more meaningful and effortless they become. In repeating prayers and rituals over and over, they become part of us, so much so we don't need to focus on words or gestures because we now "know them by heart." Prayers we were taught as children to memorize–Our Father and Hail Mary, believed to be the most powerful Christian prayers–could be repeated anytime and anywhere, making the power in prayer easily accessible. Prayers became perfect when we knew them by heart. Repetition builds up divine energy in prayers and rituals, which we tap into every time we pray, making repetition a powerful ingredient in making magic.

The most sacred and powerful rituals we know are those that have been repeated over and over for thousands of years. Like the Eucharist in Christianity, and the high holy rituals of Judaism and Islam, all repeated for thousands of years by trillions of believers, charged as they are with generations of divine energy to tap into every time we pray. The same is true in the power of mantra, litanies, ancient prayers, and rituals. We are careful to repeat the same words, use the same gestures and the same symbols, believing each holds a sacred power that builds and grows with each repetition, so much so they effect what they signify, just as they did in the beginning. Raising, folding, and extending hands in prayer; bowing and kneeling; chanting and dancing—all charge ritual with the magic power of having been repeated in prayer since the beginning of time. Sacred words, sacred gestures, and sacred objects become essential in creating the power in repetition, and all become sacred from having been prayed over for centuries.

Even with the simplest of family rituals—celebrating holidays and holy days—extra care is taken to repeat the way it was done in the beginning when something extraordinary, something meaningful happened the first time. We gather the same people on the same date, serve the same food, do the same activities, repeating everything with the hope of recreating the love and joy we know every time we gather on that day, and in that way. Even now, Christmas is not the same for me without Polish sausage, Mom's *kapusta* (sauerkraut and spareribs), herring in cream sauce, and the closest I can find to Daddy's rye bread. We rely naturally on the magic in repetition to connect with what we experienced as the best of times.

It's easy to understand how meaningful certain activities become the more we do them. Significance deepens over time in a profoundly simple, almost unconscious way; we find ourselves relying on such rituals for well-being and peace of mind. We want to wallow in the warmest of memories. We even feel out of whack when those times are missed. Those who belong to clubs understand this perfectly, as do most nuns I know, for whom sisterhood depends upon repetitive coming together to deepen the ties that bind lovingly. The annual meeting at the House of Pizza–where we hung out in school–remains a ritual of friendship shared by lifetime friends, one of whom I've known–Veronica Hargrove–since my first day of kindergarten. Getting together regularly for years is all it takes to transform strangers into friends, friends into family, women's groups into sisters. Such is the divine power in repetition to transform lives with the kind of magic we folks make.

Words have always been associated with the sacred. In Christian scripture, the Gospel of John begins with the passage "*In the beginning was the Word. The Word was with God. The Word was God.*" (John 4:4) Words carry the power of effecting what they signify. Hearing someone say "I love you" makes us feel loved. Words of hate and anger devastate just as effectively. Ordinary bread and wine become divine when we repeat the words attributed to Christ at the Last Supper: *"This is my Body.*

This is my Blood." Repeat the words prayerfully and the magic in ritual does its work. Miracles happen. It is done as we say. *Abracadabra* is one of the oldest, most repeated, and most powerful words, meaning *"I create as I speak"*–or most accurately in Hebrew, *"It came to pass as it was spoken."* Because certain words are so powerful, the repetition of those words has everything to do with the making of magic in ritual, especially combined with the divine powers in faith, necessity, and nature.

Repeating certain ritualistic gestures bears a similar divine effect. While praying, *"Kadush, Kadush, Kadush,"* Jews stand on tiptoe, lifting themselves closer to heaven. By extending our hands in prayer, we bless. By anointing the forehead with oil, or by immersing in water, we bless and baptize new life. By the laying on of hands, we heal the sick and lift depressed spirits. When we fold our hands in prayer, we point and focus our energy on the holy, and when we pray on bended knee, our soul speaks most powerfully. Such actions, repeated for thousands of years, have built up reservoirs of divine power we tap into and release every time we repeat those gestures in prayer. In preparing your rituals, therefore, integrate into everything you do the power in *belief, necessity, nature,* and *repetition.* In doing so, you connect and align yourself with all holy spirits who have uttered those words and offered those prayers for thousands of years. Once you become soulfully connected in those ways, the magic in ritual begins.

*Your daily life is your temple
and your religion.*

– KAHLIL GIBRAN

HOW TO MAKE MAGIC

Because so much of ritual's transforming power comes from what we bring to the altar, there's also a method to the magic in ritual, certain steps good to follow whenever we engage in ritual prayer. Like all steps given as guides, their soulful goodness lies in making them our own, making them a natural part of the flow with which we go every time we pray. Far more than just an outline or list of things to do, each step works in a specific way to prepare for divine intervention, to create magically favored moments, to get us ready for a visit with deities. Assuming you've heard the call to ritual prayer, created sacred space, and prepared your altar, you're now ready to begin making magic. You are all you need.

Walking you through the seven steps I follow is the best way to explain how magic works; how each step puts us more deeply in touch with the mystery and magic in ritual prayer. The amount of time spent on each step is never as important as the inner readiness to move on. Don't worry about timing; it comes naturally when you go with the flow of what happens next. Following intuition is essential, so let the holy spirit within you–the angel in your soul–be your guide. Pausing for moments of silence is also critical in ritual prayer. Once you begin and the ritual moves to take on a life of its own, be attentive to the need to pause for a moment of silence, to let yourself be led to what happens next.

Clarifying, purifying, and focusing our wishes matters most when placing them on the altar. Wherever the need for prayer comes from, never is it our job to judge its merit or significance. In the spirit world everything is holy just as it is. Whatever inner necessity calls us to ritual prayer, that's where divine activity has already begun. So never question needs for what may appear to be little things–new job, sick pet, the ability to quit smoking or lose weight–because everything in sincere hearts is precious in the sight of God, as it should be in our sight also. Purity of heart–preface to ritual prayer–is where we start. According to the Beatitudes in Christian scripture, it's what we need in order to see God. Pure how? Without wish to harm. Without hatred, anger, and need for revenge. Leave the altar and make peace first are what Christ requires if we're that angry. A firm reminder is needed to be very careful in discerning what to ask for, to purify intentions of anything negative before approaching the altar. If you're thinking of good ways to do someone in, think again. Think instead about praying all obstacles–inside and out–be removed so only good things happen through you, as well as those you'd like eliminated. Think about praying for others to be bound from hurting you or standing in the way of your success and happiness. Praying to be bound by love and protected from all harm is a good way to focus any anger or resentment that may accompany a request. It's the focus on healing, not hurting, that makes hearts and thoughts pure enough to see God.

One: Choose the Date

Once the request is clear and heart pure, decide the best time for your spells and blessings. In choosing the date, consult all calendars–lunar, astrological, seasonal, holidays, holy days, saints' feast days–and align yourself with the divine power certain days hold. The lunar calendar, for example, has always been a determining factor in my setting dates to mark holy days. Ancient ancestors understood there's something mysterious and powerful about the moon's effect. The phases of the moon not only regulate ocean tides, menstrual cycles, crop cycles, and possible UFO sightings but also affect the ups and downs of our spiritual life. Many find intuitive and psychic energy most perceptive when the moon is full, making it a perfect time to focus on attracting what we want. In a similar manner, when the moon is dark and energy low, it becomes the most oppor-tune time to remove all negative feelings and obstacles to our wish being granted. If we pay no attention to the moon at all, believing it has no influence on life whatsoever, some think that causes lunacy. So pay attention to the wisdom of every ancient religion and consult the lunar calendar when choosing the date for your spells and blessings. Magic is waiting to work extraordinary wonders on the most powerful days of the year.

Religious feasts and holy days–Easter, Passover, Ramadan, Christmas, Rosh Hashanah, New Year's Eve, solstice, and equinox–are reliably perfect times for joining in with our wishes, as they're charged with thousands of years of prayerful energy to tap into and draw upon. Aligning our prayer with the prayer of ancestors, repeating ancient words and gestures, clicking elements into place on that day, is all we need to set the stage for divine intervention. Find a date most fitting for you and your wish; then work toward aligning yourself with the divine energy already present. In Catholicism, for example, every day is perfect. Not only is there a saint named patron for every day–someone we can call upon for help–but every illness, need, or profession also has its protector saint. Everyone–and everything–has a saint attached, and praying for certain favors on certain days from certain saints is believed to be extra powerful. Every day a saint is available to be called upon for help, forever available to hear everyone's prayer.

New Year's Eve is a uniquely powerful day for ritual prayer, positioned as it is at the end of one year and beginning of a new year. Ends turn into new beginnings on this day, almost begging us to tap into its divine transforming energy. New Year's

Eve is a high holy retreat day in the convent, meaning we were wrapped in total silence, not allowed to speak until the following morning after breakfast. At first it felt like high holy torture to spend New Year's Eve in silence and not partying with reckless intoxicating abandon, but once I began writing every day–about the best and worst parts of the day–New Year's Eve became my favorite day of the year. Now it is the day to retreat and pull out all the journals of the past year, reading through day after day to find the best and hardest parts of the year. At first, lists appeared completely different with the worst being opposite the best, but over time, as it is now, the worst and best appear the same. Had it not been for some of the worst parts of the year, I never would have discovered the best of times. Every year, I look forward to the Annual Journal Review on New Year's Eve as a day of transformation, a day to let go of the year past and welcome the new year with all its opportunities, blessings, and surprises. I encourage you too to look at New Year's Eve as a uniquely powerful day for spells and blessings. Either alone or together with family and friends, it is a perfect day for thanks to be given, mistakes forgiven, and wishes made.

Because I grew up Catholic with a Communion of Saints to call upon for assistance, Feast Days have become powerful times of the year to ask for specific favors. Similarly, the particular charism of every saint lends itself to be called upon whenever we need their help. For example, the Feast of Saint Raphael, the Archangel, is September 29. As the patron saint of travelers, happy meetings, and healing, Raphael can be called upon whenever we need protection while traveling, wish for a happy meeting, or need to be healed. Saint Jude–my mother's favorite–whose feast is celebrated on October 28, is the patron of impossible causes. I'm certain he gets called upon daily for divine intervention in desperate times. Saint Rita, whose feast is May 22, is also patron of impossible causes with Saint Jude, a divine double whammy of divine power when asking for the impossible. Teresa of Avila's feast is celebrated on October 15, but as the patron of headache sufferers and writers, she too can be called upon daily, and a personal favorite, Saint Dymphna, patron of those suffering diseases of the mind, also protects us from those who drive us crazy. Her feast is celebrated on May 15. A communion of saints is available to all, believer and non-believer, in helping grant our prayers.

Other days soulfully suitable for ritual prayer are birthdays, anniversaries, dates loved ones departed this life, holy days in all our lives. Think of the holiest days in your life and begin remembering them in prayer. On those days, like all holy days, a portal to the spirit world opens, inviting us, begging us to sit for a spell and wallow in the mysteries of the day. Every day I light candles in remembering my dearly departed loved ones. On the anniversary date of their departure, in lighting a candle, I invite them to stop by for a spell and spend the day with me. Once we open the door to the spirit world in prayer, we begin to see this world more clearly. We begin to see, as Saint John Chrysostom saw, how *"those we love and lose are not where they were before; they are now wherever we are."* Once we open the door to the spirit world, a communion of saints and loved ones appears to hear our prayer. Begin calling on angels, saints, and dearly departed loved ones in rituals and prayers and you will also begin to see and feel more clearly and soulfully how truly *"they are now wherever we are,"* a thought away. Think of them and they are here. Whenever we think of dearly departed loved ones, it's because they are near and we are conscious (at some unconscious level) of their presence. Abracadabra.

All of this is to say the more divine forces we gather to work with us in spells and blessings, the more powerfully transforming results are likely to be. So, when the time comes to choose the date, take care to align yourself with all the powers in heaven and on earth. Draw upon the divine energy in the moon, sun, planets, stars, and the earth. Check out the saint for the day. Connecting with multiple sources of divine energy in our spells and blessings serves to intensify the transforming power, working most effectively in making the magic of dreams come true. Finding the most powerful day for your spells and blessings, therefore, is the first step. Once you've picked the perfect day, you are soulfully ready to make the day holy.

Two: Make Holy the Day

Once we choose the date to make magic, the day becomes holy, set apart from the rest, a day in which deities will be stopping by for a spell. O Holy Day. You wake up and the day feels different. This is the day we choose to make holy. Unlike any other day of the week, the day we choose becomes supernatural, a day for making magic, a day spent in expectation of a visit from God. From sunrise to moonrise, our wish becomes the focus, the moment for which we spend the day preparing. Spend the day envisioning your wish coming true, your prayer being answered. Trust in the word of God who reveals *"Because of your faith it will be done to you."* (Matthew 9:29) How we prepare ourselves and our homes for divine intervention has everything to do with step two: Making holy the day we choose for spells and blessings.

In making days holy, it's important to keep in mind everything is holy just as it is; no extraordinary efforts are necessary. All that's needed is a shift in consciousness, keeping in mind this is the day you selected for ritual prayer. This is the day you are expecting deities–and any other holy spirits invited–to stop by for a spell. Do whatever feels natural in preparing for divine guests. If you are accustomed to participating in religious services, there is no more fitting way to prepare for your holy day than by engaging in those sacred rituals. If you're not drawn to religious services, making the day holy begins with a prayer of thanksgiving for the day you have chosen, and a constant inner focus on what it is you want to happen. What do you wish to come true? What heartfelt prayer do you bring to the altar? Deities know what you need more than you do, so don't obsess over the right words or the perfect request. Open your soul to what the day brings and let it be.

Most important is focusing only on positive thoughts and activities, taking care to avoid anything negative, upsetting, or disturbing. Negative thoughts and feelings have no place on the altar, serving only to block and break the spell. Surround yourself on that day with the best of friends and the most comforting circumstances, focusing only on the divine visitors to come. You may choose to spend the day in solitude. Do whatever you need to do to prepare yourself for a divine visit. In seeing the day as holy, we allow into our life only what we find divine. Focus throughout the day is singleheartedly concentrated on what we want to happen. By focusing all energy on our prayer, we begin our entry into the spirit world and prepare ourselves soulfully for a visit from deities.

In addition to preparing and collecting ourselves for ritual prayer, we also need to prepare our home and altar. In advance, gather everything you need—flowers, candles, water, crystals, oils, stones, incense, photos, statues—and assemble the sacred items on the altar. The spell you choose may require additional items such as herbs, charms, cord, all assembled on the altar at this time. Clear the space from distraction, clutter, anything that may diminish focus. Housekeeping is part of making a day holy, and clearing clutter tops the list—from mind, heart, soul, and home. If possible, open windows to let in sunlight, moonlight, and fresh air. On one dark and stormy night, I let snow blow in with visiting spirits. Follow intuition and you'll know what to do to make your home and altar holy, keeping in mind everything can be made holy and nothing is inappropriate. Holy is in the eye of the beholder, and everything is holy for those who know how to see. Over time, the more you engage in ritual prayer, the more you will find yourself making every day holy. Every day, time will be set aside to sit with deities for a spell.

Whatever you need to do to make holy the day set aside for making magic, that's the next step. If others are joining you for the ritual, it's important for them to prepare in a similar manner. In extending the invitation, ask guests to keep the day holy also in whatever way they see fit. In gathering together, you may want to share a glass of wine—distilled or undistilled spirits—as a way of pulling the group together and bringing the focus to what it is the group wishes. Group members may also be asked to bring items to place on the altar, symbolizing the presence of everyone's wish. Group rituals can become very powerful in making magic with a united focus on what's wished for, as well as soulful bonds among group members being strengthened and deepened. The prayers and rituals done in the sisterhood when all are gathered become a powerful uniting force uniquely different from that experienced in solitary prayer. Either together or alone, all make a conscious effort to make holy the day chosen for ritual prayer.

If the spell is done alone at night, a long leisurely bubble bath can become the perfect preparation, as will a trip to the hot tub or a hot, steamy shower. Whatever alters your consciousness and shifts your attention to the spirit world is the perfect way to prepare for ritual prayer. Just as we spend days preparing when friends and family visit, so do we spend days preparing for a visit with deities. We want hearts and homes to be welcoming places for divine intervention. The day you choose becomes your Sabbath, your high holy day, your feast day. It becomes noticeably different from all other days in that the most important work of the day is preparing for God to stop by for a spell. Even though the day we choose may, of necessity, be full of ordinary works and distractions, they too become part of making the day holy, keeping us focused on the moment set for ritual prayer. The whole day works toward intensifying energy and charging us for making magic, making holy the moment we choose to begin.

Three: Beginning

Because the time to begin spells and blessings is entirely up to you, never underestimate the power in the hour, and the mystery in the still of the night. Finding night quieter and more enchanted, I almost always choose the darkness of night to begin spells and blessings. All ancient religions revered time as sacred. They recognized a sacred significance in the cycles of nature because they thought divine powers ruled them, believing prayer and ritual helped turn fall into winter, winter into spring, spring into summer, and summer into fall. I believe that too. Like the seasons of the year, some hours are also more naturally and divinely charged than others, perfect times to begin. It could be the hour we were born, the time loved ones departed this life, the hour children were born–all become highly charged times in ways other times are not. Give thought to the power in the hour you choose to begin your spells and blessings.

In discerning the most powerful times for ritual prayer, there's something magic in midnight on New Year's Eve, Christmas Eve, and Holy Saturday, unlike any other midnight. A New Year is born, light overcomes darkness, and life rises from the dead at midnight on those days. The same enchanted feeling comes at the winter and summer solstices, spring and fall equinoxes, and the rising of any full and new moon. Whatever time in life is marked by some personal or astrological transformation, whatever time feels magic, that hour becomes a naturally powerful time to begin spells and blessings. It all begins with you. Whatever time you choose will become the best time for your prayer. When the time is set, the invitation is sent. The deities and holy spirits you invoke will be present when you are.

Many believe there are certain times in every day–1:11, 3:33, 11:11–when the door to the spirit world opens and synchronistic events happen–magically favored moments. For example, one of my best and oldest friends, called "Bone," finds her attention shift in noticing, repeatedly and more frequently, 11:11 on clocks, restaurant checks, grocery store receipts, and the timing of text messages and emails received. Whenever we notice 11:11 or 11:11 a.m. or p.m., we think of one another and send loving thoughts. If we can make it in time, we also send an email or text – "thinking of you." I call it "Bone Time." Magic time for me also is 3:33, as though a window into the spirit world opens for a moment, an opportunity appears for divine intervention. I stop what I'm doing, make a wish, offer a prayer, and wallow in what feels like a brief shining moment of being granted peace. Waking at 3:33 a.m. is also believed to be spirit visiting time, waking just enough to remind us they are wherever we are, visiting us in dreams. So, pay attention to the times of every day. When you notice 11:11, 3:33, 11:11, or any significant time of the day for you, stop what you're doing, offer a prayer, make a wish, and be granted peace. All are perfect times for making magic.

For me–a night person–the power in the hour is almost always in the still of the night, around midnight. Day is done and New York City winds down. Today turns into tomorrow. A new day is about to be born. Everything feels more mysterious at night, including dreams, revealing the more enchanting side of darkness. Candles burn brighter. Clouds of incense rise thicker and higher, appearing more visible. Moon and one star appear. Lulu the cat becomes mellow, less chatty. And most of the world I know is asleep, leaving me in solitary splendor. Night time is naturally soul time, as though created specifically for spells and blessings, divinely designated as the perfect time to pray, also the time deities choose to visit in sleep and dreams. At night deities do their divinest work, uninterrupted. I also prefer to make magic at night.

If your days are full and busy, you may need to alter your consciousness before you begin; to shift gears from day to night and deepen focus on what it is you're praying for. Regardless of the time set for ritual prayer, a shift of focus from the outer world to the inner world is necessary. At night, a foaming hot bubble bath is my drug of choice. Running hot water, clouds of bubbles, steam heat, and candlelight–all serve to shift gears and sink into the soul where we prepare for prayer. While historically there are many effective ways to alter consciousness for ritual prayer–meditation, yoga, music, solitude, fasting–whatever way works best for you is the way to begin. Peyote is a consciousness-altering sacrament in certain Native American rituals. The point is to disconnect from the busyness of the day, collect yourself and your thoughts, and free yourself to focus exclusively on a visit from God. Whatever way you choose to shift gears and enter sacred space, however you prepare yourself to enter the spirit world, you will know instinctively when the appointed time comes to approach the altar and begin. When the door to the spirit world opens, you will feel ready to enter.

In the beginning, therefore, all you do is get yourself ready. In the same way you prepare to entertain company you've invited over for a spell, so too do you do whatever is necessary to prepare for a visit from deities, for divine intervention. What we do to prepare is as unique as we are. There is no wrong way to get ready, unless you start drumming up negative thoughts and wishes. Calming ourselves down and finding stillness within is most important. In beginning to pray, we need to be able to listen to the voice of spirits and tune in to the movements of divine activity. We need to wrap ourselves in solitude and silence. Spirts communicate through thoughts, feelings, ideas, and images, and we need to be able to discern messages. We need to silence all outer voices and tune in to the still small voice of the angel in our soul. In beginning to pray, we need most of all to prepare ourselves to listen to the voice of God, who has heard our prayer even before we've begun to ask. We need to sit down for a spell and listen.

*No one suspects the days
to be gods.*

–Ralph Waldo Emerson

Four: Candle Lighting

Most of us have been lighting candles and making wishes since our first birthday. Very early in life, we were introduced to the wish-come-true magic of candle lighting, as though there is mysterious power in fire capable of making what we want to happen. I never thought seriously about fire or its divine power, until I learned about the Vestal Virgins, ancient Rome's female priests and world's first nuns. In order to serve the goddess Vesta, the Vestal Virgins left home at an early age–some as young as six– cut their hair short, dressed in white robes, wore an ornamental headband, and promised at least thirty years of virginity. The goddess Vesta was worshipped as the guardian of home and hearth fire, divine keeper of home fires burning and hearts yearning. In her eyes, we are all Temples of Sacred Fire. A divine spark of life burns within each of us never to be extinguished.

In the Temple of Vesta, an eternal fire burned, and it was the exclusive job of the Vestal Virgins to ensure the flame never died. They tended the fire in shifts, never taking their eyes off the flame. Fire became a sacred symbol indicating the presence of Vesta. Vestal Virgins were society's keepers of the flame, and no job was more important to peace on earth than keeping the Temple Fire burning. So critical was their work, everyone believed terrible darkness and destruction would befall Rome if the flame were extinguished, even for a moment. As long as the Temple Fire continued to burn, all manner of things would be well. The contemplative work of the Vestal Virgins was so essential to the well-being of Roman society that sisters would be scourged mercilessly in public, even buried alive, if the fire went out on their shift. Keeping the Temple Fire burning was literally a matter of life and death.

What is it about tending the fire that warrants being scourged mercilessly in public and buried alive if you nod off? Why does the flame being extinguished, even for a split second, have such dire consequences for the Roman Empire? What kind of fire is this? The secret lies in the sacredness of the flame. Clearly, this is no ordinary fire. For our ancestors, and for us, fire on the altar is a sign the goddess is present. Every time candles were lit in religious rituals, those gathered around the flame entered into its transforming energy. That's a powerful way to think about fire. I looked at fire and didn't think twice. Our ancestors looked at fire and fell to their knees before the deities burning within. So too should we look at our soul, our Temple of Sacred Fire, and never let the divine spark within be extinguished. We too are called to fall on our knees before the deities living within one another. In the lighting of candles on our altar, the door to the spirit world opens, and God is present. Holy. Holy. Holy.

All primitive religions divinized fire as the most powerful symbol to express the visitation of the living God. In the course of personal dialogue with Moses, Yahweh manifests Himself in the form of a "consuming fire"; the burning bush is consumed with fire but not destroyed. God speaks in consuming fire. Other symbols–breath, water, wind–were used to translate the essence of divinity, but fire appears as the most powerful symbol to acknowledge the presence of God. In Christian scripture, at Pentecost, the Holy Spirit appears in "tongues of fire" over the heads of apostles. In every religious ritual, from the beginning of time, candles were, and still are, lit to symbolize the presence of God. In Catholic churches, prior to stricter fire codes, a "sanctuary lamp" containing a lit candle hung near the altar, never extinguished, symbolizing God was home. You were entering the House of God. Today, in preparation for most religious activities, like the Eucharist in Christianity, the first ritual act, before the priest appears at the altar, is the lighting of candles, symbolizing God is present. The ritual has begun.

Because candle lighting is such a powerful moment in initiating ritual prayer, it's good to anoint and prepare candles before lighting. Anointing objects with oil before placing them on the altar is another ancient religious tradition. Its purpose is to consecrate objects for prayer and mark the spot of divine presence. Anoint candles by rubbing scented oil (or olive oil) along the sides and top of the candle, focusing on what it is you want to happen. Carving initials, dates, or symbols on candles before anointing further enhances the ritual. In anointing with oil, we thank God for all we've been given, charge the candle with our wish, and dedicate the lighting, in gratitude for the answer to our prayer.

While intention is most powerful in lighting the candles you choose, the color of candles is believed by some to enhance the power in granting certain requests. For example, black candles are good for binding and banishing negativity; white candles enhance divination and healing; pink candles symbolize love and friendship; purple candles promote power, spirit, and wisdom; red candles symbolize love, strength, and courage; and green candles are good for luck, wealth, and fertility. I believe white candles cover all bases. Rituals are no less effective if you don't have the right color candle to match your wish. What matters most is clarity of intention and purity of heart. Without our speaking a word, deities know what we need most.

After preparing candles by anointing and charging them with your spirit, darken the room, light the candles, and focus on the circle of light within which your magic will be done. If others are joining you, now is the time for everyone to circle the altar. Either way–alone or together–candle lighting signals our spells and blessings have begun. The door to the spirit world has opened, and we have stepped into the presence of God. That's how powerful candle lighting is in beginning our spells and blessings. Divine intervention has begun. Pause for a moment of silence. Keep your eye on the flame. It signals the presence of God who is about to speak to you. Blessed Be.

Five: Incensing

Incensing follows candle lighting in these spells and blessings– the burning of incense and the appearance of thick, white clouds of sometimes intoxicating smoke. Just as God spoke from fire in biblical days, so too did deities appear frequently in clouds of smoke. Flames of fire and enveloping clouds of white smoke both signal divine intervention. Mists and clouds revealed the close proximity of God, so much so incensing became the signal for the height of religious activity. Just prior to the moment of consecration in the Catholic Mass, for example, the altar, the congregation, the deacons, and the priest are incensed with thick, mind-altering clouds of burning frankincense and myrrh, and again blessed with holy water. Then the moment of "transubstantiation" occurs, wherein bread and wine become divine, transforming the faithful who take communion into the Body and Blood of Christ. Incense and holy water serve the same divine purpose here. Clouds of smoke rising from burning incense and the blessing with holy water both signify God is present and the magic of transformation has begun. Our prayer is being heard. Blessed be.

Practically speaking, incensing involves nothing more than the burning of smudge sticks–bundles of dried sage–or scented incense. Frankincense and myrrh are my clouds of choice; sometimes sandalwood. Sage is believed to be a sacred herb of deities, making smudge sticks an excellent choice. Smudge sticks can be purchased easily, or homemade with bundled dried sage bound together tightly with string. Sage is also the magic ingredient making turkey stuffing divine. Always associated with heightening the power and mystery of religious rituals, the burning of incense or sage works to purify the sacred space and those gathered, purifying us, inside and out, enabling us to focus singleheartedly on our prayer.

Ancient religions also used incense or perfume in their rituals as a symbol of offering prayer and praise, conveying the presence of God. Temple liturgies called for an altar of perfume with censors and bowls of incense. Incense conveyed a silent vibration that breathes the essence of divinity and gives a glimpse of divine life hidden within us, a sign of God's blessing. Incense rising in smoke became a sign of the love and praise offered to the godhead, signified the adoration of God in a most pleasing way. From the beginning of time, religious rituals lit candles and burned incense to signify most powerfully the presence of God.

The smoke from incensing, like the flame in candle lighting, is meant to be as mind altering as it is purifying. Because deities are known to appear in clouds of smoke, allow the incense to clear your mind and sharpen your focus. Pass the incense around the altar and everyone present. If you are not alone, have participants incense one another. Incense is most effective in lifting our spirit from this world into the spirit world, shifting consciousness to the soul's work of making magic, clearing the way for what we wish to be granted. It's fitting at this time to pause for a moment of silence and listen for the voice of God in whose presence we stand. Just as we acknowledge the presence of any visitor who enters our home and thank them for coming, so too is it a moment of grace to acknowledge the presence of deities with a prayer of thanksgiving. Acknowledge the presence of God with loving gratitude in a moment of silence, moving forward when you feel it's time to begin.

If you are allergic or irritated by smoke and incense, sprinkling with holy water is just as effective, and can always be used with incense or without. Water is a divine symbol of the presence of God with its cleansing and purifying powers, frequently used in ancient rituals of baptism and initiation. Pour holy water into a shallow bowl or cup, and using a small branch or your hand, sprinkle everyone in your circle, as well as the altar. You may also want to anoint yourself and everyone present with holy water. Dip your thumb in holy water; then anoint your forehead, your lips, and your heart with a sign of the cross or other sacred symbol. The sign of the cross is an ancient symbol predating Christianity, a powerful gesture in ritual prayer. You and others can also be anointed with oil at this time, indicating the acceptance of your priesthood in the ritual about to begin.

Where to get holy water? From any church, if you practice a religion that uses it. Water from oceans, lakes, and streams is also holy. In the good old days, rainwater was believed to have magical power, coming as it does from heaven. Any water from sites sacred to us becomes holy, and we can make any water holy with our blessing. All you need are candles, water, salt, sunlight or moonlight, and a bell. A "Full Moon Holy Water Blessing" (p. 122) is included in this book. Again, even if you don't have all the ingredients, your intention is the magic-transforming ingredient. When it comes to ritual prayer, we are all priests and priestesses, endowed with soulful powers to make everything divine with our prayer. Whether we incense with smudge sticks, frankincense, and myrrh or sprinkle with holy water, all are ancient sacred rituals known to summon deities and welcome divine intervention.

We are at the heart of ritual's mystery now, transformation's turning point. Everything is in place. You are recollected and ready. The altar is prepared. Candles anointed and lit. Incense burning and all are anointed with oil and holy water. In pausing for a moment of silence, take deep breaths as the mind focuses with laser-like precision on the prayer being granted or the wish being made. Deities are present as you stand before them in prayer. The moment of making magic has arrived. *Abracadabra. "It comes to be as it is spoken."*

Six: Abracadabra

Surrounded by candlelight, incense, the presence of deities and holy spirits, the time has come to cast your spell, offer your prayer, make magic. This is the moment of transformation, the magic moment when what we speak and what we do happens. This is when we place our offering on the altar and let deities do their work. Whatever spell or blessing you've chosen, now is the time to cast your spell. For example, if you're doing the "Get Well Spell" (p. 233), now is the time to take white paper and in green ink write your health request. Fold the paper three times, repeating after each fold, *"As I wish, so might it be."* Then gather the eucalyptus leaves, angel charm, and crystal in the green cloth and tie three knots with blue cord, repeating after each knot, *"Blessed Be."* If you are doing the "Saint Francis Prayer for Peace" (p. 178), this is when you and those gathered with you chant or pray the Prayer of Saint Francis: *"Make me a channel of your peace...."* And if you are doing the "Saint Joseph Real Estate Spell" (p. 149), now is the time to bury his statue upside down in the backyard. Now is the time for *Abracadabra.*

Having entered the door into the spirit world, everything we do now becomes part of ritual's transforming magic; every move we make carries a divine charge. What we pray for is happening. We are clearing the way for the invisible to be made visible. It's the feeling of being connected, in touch with divine energy, transformed. What we envision is becoming real. Whatever God or divine power you call upon, whatever moves you make, whatever words you speak, whatever spell or blessing you choose, all become charged with the divine magic in ritual, working immediately in answering our prayer. Because consciousness is so highly raised at this point, even the simplest gesture, like standing on tiptoe, feels divine. We feel moved into the spirit world, and the experience is uplifting. Some refer to the "goosebump experience." Feeling moved to tears or laughter is completely normal in sacred space, so don't be surprised if your spells and blessings are full of both. Feeling deeply connected to everything, especially those gathered around the altar, is typical of the transformation experienced, oftentimes making the atmosphere delightfully fun. It feels as though what we've asked for has already been granted and no one is surprised. All these mysterious feelings are signs of divine intervention, clear indicators of the magic in ritual at work.

Paying soulful attention to where the spirit leads is very important now. Add to a spell, change something, write a prayer or poem, or chant a hymn that comes to mind. Give yourself time to pause in silence in order to hear messages from God, in whose presence you stand, in order to be moved and inspired by the holy spirits surrounding you. Pausing in silence throughout the ritual is a way of letting your spirit be moved, focusing transforming energy powerfully on the prayer you have placed on the altar. Following spell "recipes" literally is never as important as understanding what a spell does and letting your spirit show you how. The transforming power in ritual prayer comes from uniting our spirit with the divine spirits we've called upon and letting our self be led wherever the spirit goes. This is where we follow with reckless abandon whatever our spells and blessings call us to do. This is where we become transformed by such divine activity, where the magic in ritual does its work of making real what we ask for. *Abracadabra.*

Even though we may not be able to see clear results immediately, we stand in the presence of God and feel our prayer has been granted, keeping in mind any hesitation or doubt in our heart breaks the holy spirit of the spell. Doing spells and blessings with a believing heart is the most powerful *Abracadabra* of all. Here we take ordinary, everyday life, bring it into sacred space, place it on the altar, and pray it becomes all it can be. We pray to become divine and likely feel divine at this moment. Ends turn into new beginnings here, and peace comes flowing like a river even through our worst misery. All of life becomes sacred, touched by God, moving us from where we were to a more sacred place where we are granted peace. While standing in the presence of God and placing our prayer in divine hands, we cannot help but become transformed by the experience. It's difficult to explain exactly what has changed, but we feel different, soulfully better, even joyful. After the ritual is done, you may want to sit in silence for a while, abiding in the presence of God, in much the same way Christians pause for a time of silence after receiving Holy Communion. Your ritual is also Holy Communion. You have communed with deities and pause now to sit in God's presence and do nothing but abide. Stay in the moment of transformation and listen for whatever message may come. When you've reached the height of divine activity–after your ritual work is done–you will hear Mother Mary speaking *"Let it be,"* which is to say: Consider it done, now let it go. *Abracadabra: "It came to pass as it was spoken."* Your wish has been granted.

Seven: Let It Be

Letting it be has everything to do with bringing your ritual to a close and discerning what to do next. When the spell or blessing feels done, after pausing for moments of abiding silence, let it go. Place your wish in the lap of deities and let it be. Your making magic is done, and the work of letting it be begins. Let deities do their work. Let the holy spirits who surround you grant your wish. Consider your wish already granted and never question results. Don't break the spell by thinking it's taking too long, it'll never happen, or your prayer has not been heard. Deities promise whatever we ask for in prayer will come to us if we believe it already has. In its own time, in its own way, whatever we pray for will happen; it will be made manifest. But between now and then, between here and there, the last step to take in ending the ritual is the soulful task of letting it be.

In bringing spells and blessings to a close, I suggest doing so in the same way you began. Step out of the spirit world the same way you entered. Repeat the prayer or chant the hymn used in the beginning, adding a prayer of thanks to deities and holy spirits for intervening and hearing your prayer. I'm not a singer, but those who are often close with a song. Candles can be extinguished or left to burn. I prefer to let them burn. But with or without candlelight, the work is done. Transformation has occurred and whatever we prayed for is taken care of. All we do in closing a ritual is done in a spirit of thanks and letting it be. In the Catholic Mass, the priest faces the people and prays, *"The Mass is ended. Go in peace."* We too end our ritual by going in peace and letting it be. All manner of things are well.

How to let it be? I like celebrating after a good spell or blessing. If I'm alone, a snack is in order. If I'm with a group, we have dinner or dessert. Churches usually have a social–coffee and donuts–after the service. Some kind of celebration is always in order after a ritual, even if we're alone. After all, deities just visited. We just made magic. Celebrating how great we feel after is always a perfect final step of gratitude. If you're with a group, it's natural for people to talk about the experience–what happened, how they feel. It may take time to come down from the divine cloud you entered in ritual prayer, to come back to earth after time spent in the spirit world. I know no one who engaged in ritual prayer and did not feel transformed in some mysterious way by the experience. You and those with you need time to shift gears from the spirit world back to the physical world. Do whatever you need to do to make the transition graceful, peaceful, and fun.

Within four to six weeks you should begin to see signs of your wish being granted, possibly sooner. Pay attention. You'll notice something's changed, including your way of thinking about the matter in question. If you are truly letting it be, without giving it a second thought or wondering how long it will take, you will begin to see clearly how strong patience makes you–even fearless–how liberating faith is, how much peace and joy can be found in drumming up divine activity at home, and how changed your life becomes when you let it be. You may even want to empower your magic further by repeating rituals three days, seven days, or weekly on the same day for four or six weeks.

Repeating spells monthly on new moons or full moons can be particularly powerful. I suspect deities do not like being pestered by anxious prayers wondering "How long, O God, how long?" But in prayerful gestures, there is a wellspring of divine power in repetition, working to increase the probability of wishes coming true. Following the spirit will lead you to next steps as long as you trust God in letting it be.

An offering of thanks is always in order at the conclusion of ritual prayer. For me, every day becomes an open door for gratitude. It's common courtesy after a divine visit to offer thanks in kind. How? By becoming kinder, more generous, more compassionate. If you have spare change, a few bucks, give it to anyone who asks without questioning how it might be spent. Find time to listen to someone's heartache. Be more patient and accepting of those who drive you crazy. Be picky about what you think. Hate no one. Be braver and never stand silent in the face of hatred and discrimination. Volunteer to help the helpless. See in everyone the face of God. Be kind to animals. Let all the divine activity in your spells and blessings bring out all the divine activity in you. Learn to find heaven in all the hell on earth. Become an angel leading others to see for themselves how divine life can become when we invite deities to enter our home and visit for a spell.

Part Two

SPELLS, BLESSINGS, AND FOLK MAGIC

What you'll find in the pages ahead is my prayer book, a collection of favorite rituals with an explanation of how they work. I find all bases covered here, and it's my hope you do too. The most important element in creating magic is making the ritual your own, which I have done, and encourage you to do the same. Follow intuition. Read through the directions for spells and decide what works best for you. Feel free to change anything–add, take parts out, think of something better–most important is making rituals your own. Everything is holy in making magic and nothing is inappropriate when we let the spirit–the angel in our soul–guide us. Making rituals our own is what makes folk magic so powerful.

I also encourage paying attention to the critical need for *pauses of silence* in ritual prayer. Pace yourself. Give yourself time to align with the presence of deities stopping by for a spell. Keep attention focused on the sacred activity of making magic, making your wish come true. Pauses of silence allow us to hear the voice of God and be led to next steps. Moments of silence allow time to listen for the voice of God and holy spirits who communicate in thought, ideas, images, feelings, insight, under-standing, and dreams, all of which can only be heard, seen, and felt in moments of silence. In planning your spells and bless-ings, therefore, pauses for silence before, during, and after the ritual are moments full of grace.

Last but not least, I encourage you to approach all ritual prayer in a spirit of gratitude, not attitude. In the beginning, we are grateful for the presence of deities, and in the end we are grateful for whatever happened. The holy spirit of gratitude makes miracles. The spirit in which we approach the altar bears directly–positively or negatively–on the outcome. Count your blessings and have fun. Approach all prayer in a spirit of grati-tude and joy. Rituals lend themselves to playful spirits looking to engage us. It is my hope you enjoy all these spells and bless-ings as much as I do. I also hope you make your own prayer book, your own book of spells, blessing, and folk magic, bring-ing all the joy you find into this world. Meanwhile, enjoy mine.

Candle-Lighting Wish-Come-True Spell

The act of lighting a candle and making a wish is a spell and blessing all by itself. It's also a powerful way to pray when that's all the time you have. The divine power in fire and the soulful power in heartfelt wishes make this simple spell work like magic. Nature and necessity always make magic whenever we light a candle and make a wish. So whenever you hear even the faintest call to pray, light a candle and make a wish. And never light a candle, for whatever purpose, without dedicating it to someone or something, even if it's a two-word prayer of "thank you" to the deities who hear our call and appear every time we light a candle. In a similar manner, never extinguish a candle without confirming your wish with *"Amen"* or *"Blessed be."* Keep in mind every time you light a candle and make a wish you are taking part in divine activity. Deities appear to hear your prayer. You are making candle-lighting magic.

BLESSED BE

Three Kings House Blessing

This blessing is done in the home every New Year, preferably on January 6, the Feast of the Magi, who experienced an epiphany on that day. It's a perfect time to pray for a New Year epiphany in our lives also, one of the best days for blessing every day of the New Year to come. The focus of all New Year house blessings is on purifying the home of any negative energy from the year past, charging the home with the divine energy of peace and love for the year to come. This blessing is also divinely fitting when moving into a new house or apartment. In a similar manner, its purpose is to purify the space of lingering negative energy, filling the space with divine energy of all you wish to come true. Houses are sacred places for souls to be at home. It is divinely fitting at the beginning of every year to invite God home for a spell and pray for a blessing. We pray for deities to stay at home in our home, making our house their house, a place where love is shared and magic made.

ON THE ALTAR

> pin or knife for carving
> 1 white candle
> 1 green candle
> oil for anointing

incense

holy water

evergreen branch

white chalk

background music ("We Three Kings" is a favorite)

DIRECTIONS

1. CANDLE LIGHTING. Before anointing, carve the year past into the white candle and the New Year date into the green candle. If you are moving into a new home, carve the date you moved out of your previous home in the white candle and the date you move into the new home on the green candle. In anointing the white candle, focus and be grateful for the best of times in the previous year, praying for all negative energy from the worst of times to be removed. In anointing the green candle, focus with gratitude on your hope for the year to come, praying for protection from all harm. Light the candles. Pause for a moment of silence. Offer a prayer of thanksgiving for the year past and a prayer of gratitude for the year to come.

2. INCENSING. Light the incense from the green candle, allowing smoke to rise. Take the incense throughout the house, incensing the corners of each room, especially

closets and around doorways. Incense everyone and every living thing, including pets and plants. Focus on purifying your home and your life from all negative energy. Return the incense to the altar and let it burn.

3. BLESSING. Take the evergreen branch (or whatever you choose) and sprinkle holy water throughout the house, blessing the same areas you incensed, including pets, plants, and everyone present. While blessing with holy water, pray your home and all who live within be blessed and protected in the year to come. Return holy water and branch to the altar. Then take the chalk, and above the doorway to each entrance, write K+M+B+*current year*. Return chalk to the altar. Let the candles and incense burn. Your house is blessed.

4. CLOSING. In concluding the blessing, promise to make an offering of gratitude for a healthy and happy New Year: a donation of time or money to the homeless or another proportional act of kindness. Never underestimate the divine power in "Blessed Works of Mercy" (p. 153), particularly at the beginning of a New Year.

BLESSED BE

Make thine home, thine abode, where an angel would desire to visit, where an angel would seek to be a guest.

–EDGAR CAYCE, READINGS 480-20

Full Moon Holy Water Blessing

This ritual is an old folk blessing for making water holy, done best under a full moon. Ocean water, rain water, water from lakes and streams, bottled water, and even tap water become holy for ritual use. In this ritual, we honor the holiness of water.

ON THE ALTAR

> 1 bowl of water
> rock salt
> 2 white candles
> oil for anointing
> incense
> bell

Place the bowl of water and salt in the center of the altar with a candle on each side.

DIRECTIONS

1. CANDLE LIGHTING. Anoint both candles, focusing on purifying the heart and centering attention on the divine activity of making water holy. Light both candles. Pause for a moment of silence, calling on the presence of God to work through you in bringing out the holiness in water. Here you can offer a favorite prayer, poem, or song. On one occasion,

those gathered began chanting the hymn *"Peace is flowing like a river, flowing out of you and me, flowing out across the ocean, setting all the people free."* Pausing for moments of silence provides psychic space for God to speak and us to listen.

2. INCENSING. Light incense from one of the candles and let it burn, allowing smoke to rise. Take the bowl of water, hold it over the incense, focusing on the holiness in water, praying *"Blessed Be."* Do the same with a small bowl of rock salt, repeating *"Blessed Be."*

3. BLESSING. Take the bell and ring it three times over the bowl of water and three times over the bowl of salt. Then take three pinches of salt and add to the water. Extend your hands in blessing over the bowl, praying from Saint Francis's "Canticle to the Sun" (p. 167).

Praised be my God, for our sister, the moon,
and for the stars,
those You have set clear and lovely in the heavens.
Praised be my God, for our sister water,
who is life to us,
humble and precious and clean.
Praise be my God, for our brother fire,

through whom you give us light in the darkness,
He is bright and pleasant and mighty and strong.
Praise You and bless you God,
We thank you and pray to serve you with great humility.
Amen.

4. CLOSING. In closing, set the water bowl under full moon-
    light for three days–day before, day of, and day after the full
    moon. Store holy water in an airtight container, keeping it
    on the altar for spells and blessings.

BLESSED BE

New Job Spell

This spell is for the jobless and unhappily employed. Focus is on a door of opportunity opening, leading to work you love. In preparing for this spell, be very specific about what you're asking for and equally careful to remove doubt, fear, and negative feelings attached to your prayer. Doubt and fear prevent spells from making magic. Envision yourself doing work you love and focus on the job you want. The magic in this spell comes from the vision of what you're praying for and the pure belief it will come to you. Envision yourself in the new job you want and pray for your wish to be granted. New Job Spells are best done as the full moon approaches, on Sundays or Wednesdays.

ON THE ALTAR

> 5-inch circle of yellow or gold cloth
> 7 gold stars
> 7 sunflower seeds
> business cards/symbols of work wanted
> 5-inch gold cord
> resume
> pin or knife for carving
> 2 yellow candles
> anointing oil

incense

3-inch square white paper

green ink pen

DIRECTIONS

1. CANDLE LIGHTING. Before anointing, carve your initials on one candle and a symbol of the job you want on the other. While anointing with oil, envision yourself doing the work you want. Light the candles and pause for a moment of silent prayer. When you are lighting the candles, deities are present. Offer a prayer of thanksgiving.

2. INCENSING. Light the incense, passing its smoke over the items on the altar. Then take your resume or job application, hold it over the incense, and pray, *"As I wish, so might it be."* Take the business cards or symbol of the work you want, hold it over the incense, praying, *"As I wish, so might it be."* Then hold your open hands over the incense, allowing the smoke to pass through your fingers, praying for the third time, *"As I wish, so might it be. Blessed Be."*

3. THE SPELL. Take the white paper, and with the green ink pen, draw a circle in the center. Within the circle, write the job and salary you want. Fold it three times, seal with a kiss, and place in the center of the yellow cloth. Add the gold

stars and sunflower seeds, tying them together in the yellow cloth with gold cord, making your new job charm. Using the gold cord, tie three knots, repeating after each, *"Blessed Be."* Place the charm on top of your resume and "let it be" on the altar. Keep candles lit.

4. CLOSING. Before bedtime, or if candles need to be extinguished, do so while praying, *"As I wish, so might it be. Blessed Be."* Place the charm under your pillow for nine nights, praying your dream comes true. If you have job interviews during that time, take the charm with you. If it's a job you want, leave a gold star and a sunflower seed behind. If not, just leave. After nine days, sprinkle the charm contents near the work you want. Bury the white paper nearby as well. Keep the charm cloth and gold cord in a sacred place for future job magic.

BLESSED BE

Memorare

This ancient Catholic prayer, known by heart, has been repeated by generations for centuries. Mary is known to grant all requests. As children, we were told by saintly nuns, *"If you don't get what you want from God, go to the Mother of God."* This prayer is charged with divine energy, believed to grant instant peace, also a soothing sedative on sleepless nights.

Remember, O Most Gracious Virgin Mary,
never was it known
that anyone who fled to your protection,
implored your help,
or sought your intercession
was left unaided.
Inspired with this confidence,
I fly unto you,
O Virgin of Virgins, my Mother.
To you do I come,
Before you I stand.
O Mother of the Word Incarnate,
in your mercy,
hear and answer me.
Amen.

BLESSED BE

Blessed Mother Broken Heart Blessing

Whatever the cause, few things in life need blessing more than a broken heart. Soulful breaks long for the kind of relief only Blessed Mothers can provide. In times that try the soul, the lighting of a candle can be a healing blessing in itself, as are favorite prayers, psalms, poems, and other sacred writings known to bear healing power. As Catholics, we grew up knowing no one knows what broken hearts feel like more than the Blessed Mother, the Mother of God; and whether we are Catholic or not, Mary never says no to broken hearts. This blessing calls on the Mother of God, and Mother of our Soul, to heal our broken heart and grant us peace.

ON THE ALTAR

statue/icon/image of the Virgin Mary

3 blue candles

4 white candle

pin or knife for carving

anointing oil (rose scented)

incense

white felt heart, cut in half

needle and blue thread

recording of Schubert's "Ave Maria"

Place the Virgin Mary statue or image in the center of the altar. In front, make a triangle with the blue candles, placing the white candle in the middle.

DIRECTIONS

1. CANDLE LIGHTING. Before anointing the blue candles, carve the word "HOLY" on each. Anoint all three with oil, focusing on all sadness and heartache being comforted. Carve your name into the white candle, and while anointing, focus on opening your broken heart to Mary's healing power. Light the three blue candles, pause for a moment of silence, and then pray the "Memorare" (p. 128).

2. INCENSING. Light the incense from the blue candle at the top of the triangle. Hold the white candle over the incense, breathe in the smoke, and focus on Mary's healing power moving through you. Do the same, holding both halves of the white felt heart over the incense, focusing on Mary binding your broken heart with love. Pause for a moment of silence. Schubert's "Ave Maria" works magic here.

3. BLESSING. Light the white candle, representing you, from the top blue candle, praying, *"As I pray, so might it be, Blessed Mother come to me."* Then take the two halves of the white felt heart and stitch them together with blue thread,

repeating with each stitch, *"Blessed Be."* Leave the stitched heart on the altar with incense and candles burning until bedtime.

4. CLOSING. Let the candles burn until they extinguish. Before bedtime, take the felt heart, hold it over the altar, and repeat the "Memorare." Place the felt heart under your pillow for nine days, praying the "Memorare" every night before bedtime. After nine days, bury the felt heart in a flower garden or a household plant, humming Schubert's "Ave Maria."

BLESSED BE

Lucky Winner Gambling Spell

This spell was revealed by a woman sitting next to me in a New Orleans casino, learned from her grandmother and handed down through generations. She won $2,500. She said it also works "really good" at Church Bingo and should be done five minutes before departing for any gambling adventure. I also have a testimonial from my best friend since kindergarten, Veronica Hargrove. Before departing for a casino trip, she did this spell and won $5,000. Our mutual best friend, "Bone," won $500, which her husband used to buy a new toilet.

Take a green candle and carve dollar signs on all sides. Light the candle, make a wish to win, let it burn for five minutes, and then blow it out. Rub your hands in the smoke, envisioning money coming to you in whatever game you play. Don't wash your hands until after gambling. Keep the candle on your altar for future use. It also enhances good luck to share your winnings to the charity of your choice. The law of Karma guarantees it will come back to you ten times over.

BLESSED BE

Problem-Solving Spell

Nothing brings us to our senses–or our knees–more than a soul-stunning problem. Every religion reveals there's nothing deities are drawn to more instantly than those who cry for help. This spell is designed for those times we don't know what to do, times when we pass through life's "cloud of unknowing." All problems come with a purpose, bearing messages we need to receive in order to move forward. The focus of this spell is on clarity of vision and insight, becoming still enough to hear the voice of God speak through intuition, asking conscience to be our guide. In doing this spell, we pray to see next steps clearly and ask for grace to be led by holy spirits, to move forward in ways revealing our best self. It's best done before bedtime, in preparation for deities to visit and speak in our dreams. Sleeping on it is an important part of the magic in this spell.

ON THE ALTAR

pin or knife for carving
˧ brown candle
anointing oil
incense
˧ bay leaf
pen

DIRECTIONS

1. CANDLE LIGHTING. Carve the name (or symbol) of the problem into the candle and anoint. While anointing with oil, focus on rubbing away the problem and seeing a resolution more clearly. Envision receiving a message about next steps in your dreams. Light the candle and pray "Litany of Holy Spirits" (p. 135). If you know another favorite prayer, this is the perfect time. Or, sit in silence. Deities know what we need.

2. INCENSING. Light the incense and hold the candle over the smoke, envisioning a resolution to the problem and pray three times, *"As I see, so might it be."*

3. SPELL. Take the bay leaf and write the name of the problem on one side and your name on the other side. Place it under the candle and let it be.

4. CLOSING. At bedtime, either let the candle burn or extinguish it, praying, *"Blessed Be."* Place the bay leaf under your pillow for three days. On the third day, crumble the leaf and scatter at the site of the problem. Mondays and Tuesdays are best for problem-solving spells, as are new moons. Remember: Problems are messages.

BLESSED BE

Litany of Holy Spirits

Holy Mother
Loving Father
Creator Spirit
Angels of God
Communion of Saints
Mother Earth
Spirit Wind
Departed Loved Ones
Enlightening Darkness
Clouds of Unknowing
Star of Hope
Mother Ocean
Holy Spirit of Sunrise
Holy Spirit of Sunset
Dark Nights of the Soul
Gods of the Universe
Guides of my Spirit
Holy Mother
Holy Mother
Holy Mother
Grant us Peace.
Hear my Prayer.

BLESSED BE

Morning Prayer

A one-hundred-year old Benedictine nun, Sister Suzanne Helmin, gave me this prayer one week before she departed this life blissfully. As she spoke, I wrote it on a napkin. It was her life's morning prayer and has become mine.

MAKE ME A BLESSING

My God,
Make me a blessing.
Those that I meet,
Make me a blessing.
As I walk down the street,
Make me a blessing.
At work and at home,
Make me a blessing.
Wherever I roam,
Make me a blessing,
That people may see
I am a blessing
For you are with me.

BLESSED BE

Happy Birthday Spell

One of the best times for a spell is your birthday, anyone's birthday, including pets. The day we entered this life is full of magic begging to be tapped into every time we end one year and begin another. Celebrating the date you were born is the heart and soul of this spell, as well as the perfect gift to yourself in honor of your birth. Birthday spells are always done on your birthday, or the birthday of loved ones, preferably, but not necessarily, at the exact time of birth. You may consider consulting an astrologer about your Solar Return, where the sun was on the day you were born, your "real" birthday. Either way, your intention to celebrate the day you were born matters most. Give yourself a party and enjoy this spell.

ON THE ALTAR

little red charm bag
3 pennies
3 sunflower seeds
charm or symbol of your wish
fresh flowers
2 candles (favorite color)
pin or knife for carving
anointing oil

incense and/or holy water
3-inch square white paper
red ink pen

DIRECTIONS

1. CANDLE LIGHTING. Place the charm bag in the center of the altar with items on top and a candle on either side. Before anointing candles, carve your birthdate and time on one and your name on the other. While anointing, focus on gratitude for the best and hardest times of the past year, acknowledging the wisdom granted in both. In lighting the candles, make your wish for the new year. Pause for a moment of silence and envision your wish coming true. Pray the "Canticle to the Sun" (p. 167), or personal prayer.

2. INCENSING. Light the incense, passing its smoke over the charm bag and charms. If using holy water, sprinkle the items and the bag, focusing on clearing the way for your birthday wish to come true.

3. THE SPELL. Make the wish. Take the white paper, and on one side, in red ink, draw a circle. Within the circle, write one word describing the best part of the year past and one word describing the hardest part of the year past. On the other side, draw a heart, and within the heart, write your

wish for the year to come–your birthday wish. Fold the paper three times, repeating with each fold, *"As I wish, so might it be. Blessed be."* Seal it with a kiss. Place the folded wish, pennies, sunflower seeds, and charms into the charm bag, and leave on the altar with candles burning. Sing "Happy Birthday" to yourself.

4. CLOSING. Allow candles to burn until extinguished, or extinguish them while praying *"Blessed be."* Place the charm bag under your pillow for nine days, repeating before sleep, *"Into your hands I commend my spirit."* After nine days, remove the folded paper and bury where flowers grow. Scatter the seeds and pennies in front of a church or favorite place. Carry your charm with you, or leave it on the altar, reminding you birthday magic is at work.

BLESSED BE

Sisters' Happy Birthday Blessing

This nun birthday blessing takes place after dinner around the lighting of candles on the birthday cake. There is one candle on the cake for everyone present. Taking turns, everyone lights a candle, making a wish for the celebrant, who lights the last candle and makes her wish. After a rowdy round or two of the "Nun Birthday Song," the celebrant extinguishes all the candles with one blow. Making wishes for one another when lighting candles is an ancient divine birthday blessing all its own. Try it and see for yourself how blessed you feel surrounded by the wishes of those who love you.

NUN BIRTHDAY SONG (Make up your own tune.)

A Happy Birthday
we sing to you,
a Happy Birthday
with good wishes too...
A Happy Birthday
From the heavens ab-o-o-o-o-o-o-o-o-o-v-e,
May Our Lady smile on you the whole year through.
Happy Birthday.

BLESSED BE

Saint Jude Blessing for the Impossible

Saint Jude is the patron saint of desperate cases, lost causes, and impossible requests. When desperation fills the soul and you don't know where to turn, Saint Jude is your spirit guide. He is known as the Saint of the Hopeless and Patron Saint of the Impossible. In repeating the "Prayer to Saint Jude," you connect with the spirit of all desperate souls who have spoken this prayer for centuries and received hope. The power in this prayer is capable of bestowing instant relief for those who believe. The feast of Saint Jude is celebrated on October 28.

PRAYER TO SAINT JUDE

> *Most Holy Apostle Saint Jude, faithful friend of Jesus,*
> *we honor and invoke you as the patron of hopeless cases and*
>   *things despaired of.*
> *Pray for me who am needy; make use, I beg you,*
> *of that particular privilege accorded to you*
> *to bring visible and speedy help*
> *where help is almost despaired.*
> *Come to my assistance in this great need*
> *that I may receive the consolations and help of heaven*
> *in all my necessities, tribulations, and sufferings,*
> *particularly* (mention your need here),

that I may bless God with you for all eternity.
I promise you, O Blessed Jude,
to remain ever mindful of this great favor,
and I will never cease to honor you
as my special and powerful patron,
and to do all in my power to encourage devotion to you.
Amen.

BLESSED BE

Money Magic Spell

The focus of this spell is on getting money. Because I know few who have too much, I frequently receive calls for money spells and prayers. The focus here is not on the lack of money–which we know all too well–but on the richness of life and the money you envision manifesting in kind. In working this spell, draw on the richness of your life and count blessings. The magic power in this spell is feeling rich in spirit and confident of the richness being made visible in the appearance of money. Among those who use this spell, it's become a favorite, and it's fun. Male or female, you get to make a doll. Money spells are best done under a full moon.

ON THE ALTAR

- 12-inch square green cloth
- dollar bills or play paper money
- white thread
- 3 silver coins
- 1 whole nutmeg
- 8-inch gold cord
- 3-inch square white paper
- 12-inch square white cloth
- 2 green candles

pin or knife for carving

anointing oil (eucalyptus)

incense/holy water

green ink pen

gold glitter

DIRECTIONS

1. MAKE THE DOLL. Take the green material and cut out a 6-inch doll figure. Stuff it with dollar bills or play money. Stitch it up clockwise with white thread, repeating with each stitch, *"As I wish, so might it be. Blessed be."* The doll represents you, so don't hesitate to add personal touches. Place the doll, along with the coins, nutmeg, gold cord, and white paper on the white cloth in the center of the altar. Set the green candles on each side.

2. CANDLE LIGHTING. Before anointing, carve dollar signs along the sides of both candles, adding the amount you're envisioning. Anoint both candles, focusing on money coming to you soon. Light both candles and pause for a moment of silence. Open with my version of the "Holy Mother Prayer," an ancient goddess prayer used for spells and blessings (or your favorite prayer).

O Holy Mother,
to You I pray,
come and grant my prayer this day,
all in true accord with Thee,
as I pray, so might it be,
(Make request here.)
Blessed Be.

3. INCENSING. Light incense from the flame of the candles, allowing smoke to rise. Take the doll, holding it over the smoking incense. While doing so, give the doll your name (or the name of one in need of money), repeating, *"I name you ____. You will always have more than enough."* Put the doll back on the white cloth and sprinkle with gold glitter. If using holy water, sprinkle and bless the doll.

4. THE SPELL. Take the white paper, and in green ink, write the amount you're requesting. Fold the paper three times, repeating with each fold, *"As I pray, so might it be. Blessed be."* Seal it with a kiss and place it on the white cloth with the doll. Fold everything together in the white cloth and tie in three knots with gold cord, repeating after each, *"Blessed Be."* Pause for a moment of silence, envisioning richness

filling your life. Extend your hands–as if to catch blessings–
and offer a prayer of thanksgiving. Let it be.

5. CLOSING. In closing, either let the candles burn out, or
   extinguish, repeating the "Holy Mother Prayer," or prayer
   used in the beginning. Take the doll charm and hide it in a
   dark place (closets are good), keeping it there until money
   arrives and your wish comes true. After receiving money,
   remove the charm, put it on the altar, and do a Thanksgiving
   Spell of your own making. Bury the white paper in a flower
   bed. Carry the silver coins with you in your wallet. Keep the
   nutmeg and doll on the altar for future use–a reminder of
   your power in making money magic.

BLESSED BE

Hail Mary

This ancient Catholic prayer honors Mary, Mother of God. When we are praying the rosary, it is repeated fifty-three times. When we were children, it was the first prayer we memorized to know by heart, and has been prayed for centuries by generations of Catholics and non-Catholics alike. So fully charged is this prayer with divine energy, it bestows blessing on all who pray:

Hail Mary, full of grace,
The Lord is with thee.
Blessed are thou among women,
And blessed is the fruit of your womb, Jesus.
Holy Mary, Mother of God,
Pray for us now
and at the hour of our death.
Amen.

Holy Mother

This prayer is inspired by an ancient divinely charged Goddess Prayer, frequently used in spells and blessings.

O Holy Mother,
To You I pray,
come and grant my prayer this day,
all in true accord with Thee,
as I pray, so might it be
(Make request here.)
Blessed Be.

BLESSED BE

Saint Joseph Real Estate Spell

Along with being the divine protector of peace in the home, Saint Joseph–spouse of Mary and stepfather of Jesus–also has a divine reputation for granting all requests having to do with selling and finding a happy home. I have a litany of testimonies documenting the remarkable success of this spell, including my own to find an affordable apartment in New York City where I could live forever. Thank you, Saint Joseph, best real estate agent I know. This spell works miracles in finding happy homes.

ON THE ALTAR

> Saint Joseph statue (dashboard size is fine)
> brown paper (big enough to wrap statue)
> 3-inch square white paper
> white cord or string
> 2 brown candles
> pin or knife for carving
> anointing oil (sandalwood incense)
> evergreen branch (or any small tree branch)
> holy water

Place brown paper in the center of the altar, with statue, white paper, and cord on top. Set one candle on each side.

DIRECTIONS

1. CANDLE LIGHTING. Before anointing candles, carve the address of the place you want on one candle and the place you're leaving on the other. While anointing, envision the place you want, and while lighting, pray the "Prayer to Saint Joseph."

   God, in your infinite wisdom and love,
   You chose Joseph to be the husband of Mary, the Mother of
   your Son.
   May we have the help of his prayers in heaven in granting my
   request here,
   and enjoy his protection on earth. We ask this through Christ
   and Mary,
   Amen.

2. BLESSING. With the evergreen branch, sprinkle and bless with holy water all the items on the brown paper, focusing on all obstacles being removed to buying, selling, and finding what you want.

3. SPELL. On the white paper, write the address of the house you want to buy, sell, or find, and the buying/selling price. Fold the paper three times, repeating with each fold, *"Saint Joseph, come to me, as I wish, so might it be."* Tape the folded

white paper to the bottom of the statue. Wrap the statue in brown paper, tying with white cord in three knots, repeating three times *"Blessed be."* If you have a yard, bury the statue upside down in the direction of where you want to move. Basements and closets are equally effective. Either way, it should be a dark, hidden location, undisturbed by ordinary activity. Prayers, spells, and blessings do their best work in the dark where we can't see and interfere. Bury the statue and let it be.

4. CLOSING. In extinguishing the candles, or letting them burn, repeat the "Prayer to Saint Joseph" used in the beginning; then let it be. Repeat the "Prayer to Saint Joseph" every day until your wish is granted. Once your prayer is answered, remove the statue from the dark and keep Saint Joseph in the kitchen or on the altar, reminding you of his power, and yours, to find and make happy homes. It is also fitting to offer a token of gratitude, paying forward what you have received. Making a donation to the homeless or shelters is always a divine gesture, as is passing along this spell to all who want to find, buy, or sell a new home.

BLESSED BE

SHIRLAPALOOZA

This is a ritual for a happy death, which my mother, Shirley, experienced in 2013 at the age of ninety. In the year before she departed this life, when the end became clear, my mother talked freely and frequently about what she did and didn't want when she died. She wanted no church, no memorial, no funeral home or cemetery, and my favorite, "NO BOO-HOOING!" She proclaimed often, "When I'm dying, I want no boo-hooing. I don't want you to mourn my death; I want you to celebrate my life." She left money for a big party with open bar, Polish wedding food (sausage, sauerkraut, mashed potatoes, gravy, roast beef, string beans/bacon, tossed salad), and a table of her favorite desserts with "a pyramid of Krispy Kreme donuts in the center."

Her wish was granted. A church hall was rented for a SHIR-LAPALOOZA with all of the above. Nearly two hundred people came to celebrate her life; enjoy a reunion of old friends and neighbors; and feast on the open bar, Polish wedding food, and favorite desserts. There were happy tears, no boo-hooing tears. Everyone spoke about wanting the same—a party to celebrate their life rather than a ritual to mourn their death. In thinking of what you'd like loved ones to do when you depart this life, consider a party to celebrate your life. Create your own SHIR-LAPALOOZA. The magic is in making it your own. The best way to have a happy death is to celebrate the life we've lived.

Blessed Works of Mercy

In growing up Catholic, we learned about ordinary works anyone can do that bestowed blessings on the giver and receiver. All that's necessary for these works is a compassionate heart and an attentive spirit. Everyday life is the altar for these spells and blessings, all called "Works of Mercy." In having mercy on others, we are granted mercy. We were taught "Corporal Works of Mercy" and "Spiritual Works of Mercy"—works that care for the body and works that care for the soul. In these soulful works, we are called to be merciful. The world is full of those in need of mercy, and we never need to go far to find them. When the whole world cries out for mercy, souls cry out to take up the work of being merciful. We are called to lives full of merciful spells and blessings.

CORPORAL WORKS OF MERCY

Feed the hungry.
Give drink to the thirsty.
Clothe the naked.
Offer shelter to the homeless.
Care for the sick.
Visit the imprisoned.
Honor the dead.

SPIRITUAL WORKS OF MERCY

Teach the uneducated.

Counsel the confused.

Offer compassion to those who do wrong.

Bear unkindness patiently.

Forgive offenses willingly.

Comfort the afflicted.

Pray for the living and the dead.

BLESSED BE

Ten-Cent Christmas Tree Blessing

Years ago I found this blessing on an old holy card at the local flea market. It cost ten cents. Every cut-down tree should be so blessed. That was my thought then, and now. While intended specifically to honor Christmas trees, this blessing is fitting for every tree, especially the sick and dying. I believe everything in nature has a soul, and every tree, in blessing our lives with everlasting beauty, deserves to be blessed as well.

BLESSING OF A CHRISTMAS TREE

God of all creation,
we praise you for this tree,
which brings beauty and memories
and the promise of life to our home.
May your blessings be upon
all who gather around this tree,
all who keep the Christmas festival by its lights.
We wait for the coming of Christ,
the days of everlasting justice and peace.
You are our God, living and reigning,
forever and ever.
Amen.

BLESSED BE

Safe Travel Blessing

It's a tradition in the sisterhood to bless and pray for those who travel. I believe that's the reason you rarely, if ever, hear news about nuns being killed in travel-related accidents. The blessings and prayers of the sisterhood protect us. You can do this simple blessing for yourself and loved ones who travel, beginning the night before departure and ending the day of safe return.

ON THE ALTAR

> pin or knife for carving
> 1 white candle
> holy water
> incense
> anointing oil
> plane ticket (or car keys if driving)
> house keys
> itinerary

DIRECTIONS

Before anointing, carve into the candle your destination as well as your home address. Anoint, light, and pray the nun prayer before a journey.

PRAYER BEFORE A JOURNEY

In the way of peace and prosperity, may God,
the almighty and merciful,
direct our steps.
May angels accompany us on the way,
that we may return home
in peace, safety, and joy.

Light incense from the candle and pass its smoke over the travel items on the altar, envisioning a safe and happy trip. Sprinkle holy water on the items as well, repeating, *"As I pray, so might it be. Blessed be."* Leave items on the altar until the following morning. When extinguishing the candle, repeat the "Prayer before a Journey," keeping in mind you are now surrounded and protected by angels. Light a candle and repeat the prayer daily until the traveler returns home "in peace, safety, and joy."

BLESSED BE

Lakeside Turning Point Spell

This ritual is based on one enacted years ago on the shores of Lake Michigan under a full moon on August 15, a high holy day for Catholics celebrating the Assumption of Mary into Heaven. For some nuns, including me, it's an extra high holy day because we professed vows on August 15. All in all, a day highly charged with the divine energy of life-changing turning points. Being assumed into heaven on earth was our prayer that day. Everyone stood at the same turning point. We entered the sisterhood together, became best friends, and were being sent to work all over the country. The focus was on blessing one another's hopes and dreams for the years to come. This blessing can be adapted to any of life's turning points, always best done under a full moon, on the shore of lakes, streams, or oceans.

The ritual began at sunset on the beach between dinner and dessert. At the first sign of moonrise, we felt ready to begin. A large circle was leveled and cleared in the sand, with a campfire altar built in the center. While the fire was built and started, others gathered gifts from the lake to surround the fire–stones, shells, driftwood, bowls of lake water, a branch for blessing, and a branch for candle lighting.

Each one brought a white votive candle, anointed and prepared in advance with initials and birth date. We made little tin-foil boats, which worked perfectly for candle floating. Everyone brought a symbol of hopes and dreams for the years to come. For example, with the wild dream of living in New York City and becoming a writer, I brought a blank sheet of white paper with hand-drawn Statue of Liberty. Everyone circled around the fire with candle and symbol of hope for the future.

We began chanting a song to Mary known by heart – "Ave Maris Stella" ("Hail O Star of the Sea").

Ave Maris Stella,	*Hail Thou Star of ocean,*
Dei Mater Alma,	*Portal of the sky!*
Atque Semper Virgo,	*Ever Virgin Mother*
Felix Coeli Porta.	*Of the Lord Most High.*
Laudate, Laudate, Laudate,	*Praise, Praise, Praise,*
Maria.	*Mary*

As we passed lake water and blessed one another, round after round was chanted until all were sprinkled and blessed. What followed became spontaneous as we each took the burning stick from the fire, lit our candle, talked about our hope for the years to come, and placed a symbol of hope in the tinfoil boat around the fire. After all was said and done (with great laughs), we each took our candle boat, made a wish, walked to the shore, setting wish-come-true candle boats off to sea.

Perfect wind blew them into moonbeams on the water. O Holy Night.

The ritual concluded with dessert–s'mores–under the full moon and star-studded sky, wallowing in the best of times. Everyone got their wish. Mine took twelve years, but it's still coming true.

BLESSED BE

Ancestor Blessing

This blessing calls us to revere dearly departed ancestors in the holy spirit of our nation's most ancient ancestors. In believing the veil between this world and the spirit world is exceptionally thin, and our dearly departed loved ones remain with us wherever we are, great comfort is bestowed upon us in praying this ancient blessing. (Blessing written by Mary Elizabeth Frye in 1932.)

I GIVE YOU THIS ONE THOUGHT

I give you this one thought to keep,
I am with you still–I do not sleep.
I am a thousand winds that blow,
I am the diamond glints on snow.
I am the sunlight on ripened grain,
I am the gentle autumn rain.
When you awaken in the morning's hush,
I am the swift, uplifting rush
Of quiet birds in circled flight.
I am the soft stars that shine at night.
Do not think of me as gone–
I am with you still–
In each new dawn.

BLESSED BE

Litany of the Blessed Mother

Deeply embedded in Catholic spirituality is the chanting of litanies, consisting of a series of petitions and responses. In public worship, the right side of the community chanted the petition, and the left side responded with *"ora pro nobis" ("pray for us").* Litanies were accompanied by thick clouds of incense burning throughout the prayer. The Litany of the Blessed Mother remains my favorite. More than any other form of prayer, litanies are rich in imagery, as if language must take leaps into poetry to express what's intended. We prayed this litany so often I came to know it by heart, remembering it still as we chanted in Latin, then years later in English.

I find the mind-altering power of repetition intensified in litanies. Shrouded in clouds of incense, a rhythm builds between the chanting of petition and response, taking on a life of its own. As is true with all religious chant, the effect becomes otherworldly, out of body, where all we know is the prayer we offer and joy in the presence of God. Because the Latin version of the Litany of the Blessed Mother is as enchanting as the English, I want you to see and hear both. Light a candle and call on the Blessed Mother to stop by for a spell. Pray to her with this litany.

LITANY OF THE BLESSED MOTHER

Sancta Maria	*Holy Mary*	*Pray for Us*
Sancta Dei Genetrix	*Holy Mother of God*	*Pray for Us*
Sancta Virgo Virginum	*Holy Virgin of Virgins*	*Pray for Us*
Mater Christi	*Mother of Christ*	*Pray for Us*
Mater Divinae Gratiae	*Mother of Divine Grace*	*Pray for Us*
Mater Amabilis	*Mother Most Amiable*	*Pray for Us*
Mater Admirabilis	*Mother Most Admirable*	*Pray for Us*
Mater Boni Consilii	*Mother of Good Counsel*	*Pray for Us*
Mater Creatoris	*Mother of Our Creator*	*Pray for Us*
Mater Salvatoris	*Mother of Our Savior*	*Pray for Us*
Virgo Prudentissima	*Virgin Most Prudent*	*Pray for Us*
Virgo Veneranda	*Virgin Most Venerable*	*Pray for Us*
Virgo Potens	*Virgin Most Powerful*	*Pray for Us*
Virgo Clemens	*Virgin Most Merciful*	*Pray for Us*
Virgo Fidelis	*Virgin Most Faithful*	*Pray for Us*
Speculum Justitiae	*Mirror of Justice*	*Pray for Us*

Sedes Sapientiae	*Seat of Wisdom*	*Pray for Us*
Causa Nostra Laetitae	*Cause of Our Joy*	*Pray for Us*
Vas Spiritualae	*Spiritual Vessel*	*Pray for Us*
Rosa Mystica	*Mystical Rose*	*Pray for Us*
Foederis Arca	*Arc of the Covenant*	*Pray for Us*
Janua Coeli	*Gate of Heaven*	*Pray for Us*
Stella Matutina	*Morning Star*	*Pray for Us*
Salun Infirmorum	*Health of the Sick*	*Pray for Us*
Refugium Peccatorum	*Refuge of Sinners*	*Pray for Us*
Consolatrix Afflictorum	*Comforter of the Afflicted*	*Pray for Us*
Regina Angelorum	*Queen of Angels*	*Pray for Us*
Regina Prophetarum	*Queen of Prophets*	*Pray for Us*
Regina Sanctorum Omnium	*Queen of All Saints*	*Pray for Us*
Regina Pacis	*Queen of Peace*	*Grant Us Peace*

BLESSED BE

Home Blessing of New Babies

In every culture, since the beginning of time, the birth of a baby is honored as a sacred event. A new person has entered our family, bringing joy to the world, changing our lives forever. We long to ritualize that moment because every culture has its ancient rites of initiating, baptizing, welcoming the child into the family, with friends promising lifelong support. Long before religion organized churches, the ritual of baptizing newborns happened, and still happens, in the home. Increasingly, family and friends are called to preside over a newborn blessing at home with family and friends. Parents plan the event, usually including a meal and party after the ritual. The person asked to preside plans the ritual and brings the supplies (oil, water, candle, linens). The ritual begins thirty minutes before the meal.

Gather everyone around the parents, who hold the baby, with grandparents and godparents standing beside them. On a linen-covered table, place a small bowl with oil, small bowl with holy water, commemorative white candle, and hand towel. The father holds the child. The ritual begins when the mother lights the candle and thanks everyone for welcoming a new life into the family and giving their blessing of lifelong support.

You'll know the best way to proceed. I invite the mother to anoint the child with oil–head, heart, hands, feet–as she blesses her child with first and middle name. She holds the child as the father pours warm water over the head and blesses the child with the family name. Grandparents and godparents anoint the baby in giving their blessing; then everyone is invited to anoint the baby's forehead and give their blessing. Because this ritual happens at home, with family and friends, the ritual will take on a life of its own, and you will know exactly what to do. Keep the candle lit while everyone remains, signifying the presence of deities with you. Most important here is opening the door for parents to baptize their own child and loved ones to give the child their blessing and promise of lifelong support. The home becomes sacred when our children are baptized where they live. The holy spirits we call upon to bless the child remain, also promising lifelong support. When we take "religion" back into our homes and hands, divine activity is inevitable. There is nothing a new soul needs more when entering this life than our blessing. And there is no better place to welcome a new soul into the family than home sweet home.

BLESSED BE

Canticle to the Sun

This blessing is believed to be a favorite prayer of Saint Francis of Assisi, as well as every generation of devotees since. A powerful prayer of praise, it's a perfect blessing at the beginning of the day, the end of the day, and every other time we feel moved to offer thanks for being alive. Cat Stevens's song "Morning Has Broken" is another canticle of praise suitable for opening prayers when lighting candles.

CANTICLE TO THE SUN

O Most Loving God,
to You belong praise, honor, and all blessing.
Praised be my God, with all your creatures,
especially our brother, the sun,
who brings us the day and brings us the light:
Fair is he and he shines with a very great splendor.
O God, the sun signifies You to us.
Praised be my God, for our sister, the moon,
and for the stars,
those you have set clear and lovely in the heavens.
Praised be my God, for our brother, the wind,
and for air and clouds, calm and all weather,
by which you uphold life and all creation.

Praised be my God, for our sister water,
who is life to us,
humble and precious and clean.
Praised be my God, for our brother fire,
Through whom you give us light in the darkness.
He is bright and pleasant and enlightening and strong.
Praised be my God, for our Mother the earth,
She who sustains us and keeps us,
and brings forth fruit and flowers of many colors, and grass.
Praised be my God, for all who pardon one another for love's
*   sake,*
and who endure weakness and suffering.
Blest are they who peacefully endure,
for you, my God, will give them rest and grant them peace.
Praised be my God, for our sister, the death of the body,
from which no one escapes.
Blest are they who die in your sight,
for death shall have no power to do them harm.
Praise you and bless You God,
we thank you and pray to serve you
with love and great humility.
Amen.

BLESSED BE

*Preach the Gospel at all times
and only when necessary
use words.*

–SAINT FRANCIS

Prayer for the Right Attitude

In Christian scripture, in the story of a "Sermon on the Mount," Christ reveals the right attitudes–Beatitudes–of those whose lives are blessed. Whenever we feel thrown off center and disoriented, it's easy for our vision of the world to reflect how we feel, sinking us into attitudes that don't feel good. We become judgmental and vindictive, wanting to do to others all the wrong they've done to us–an eye for an eye, tooth for a tooth. We know how unsettling those attitudes can be, how wrong they feel, and how unblessed our lives become as a result, full of misery. The attitudes we want to be in our life are those revealed in the Beatitudes. Whenever I feel as though I'm slipping away from my very best self, I light a candle, pray the Beatitudes, and find myself pulled back into the center of my soul where right attitudes become me. I pray you find the same.

BEATITUDES

> *Blessed are the poor in spirit, God is theirs.*
> *Blessed are the brokenhearted, they shall be consoled.*
> *Blessed are the lowly, they shall be lifted up.*
> *Blessed are those who hunger and thirst for justice, they shall*
> *   be satisfied.*
> *Blessed are the pure of heart, they see God.*

Blessed are the peacemakers, they shall be called people of God.
Blessed are those who suffer persecution for justice's sake,
theirs is the kingdom of heaven.
Blessed are you when they insult you and persecute you
and utter every kind of slander against you–
Be glad and rejoice for your reward is great in heaven.

   (Matthew 5:3–12)

BLESSED BE

Best Friends New Year's Eve Spell

This spell was put together as a New Year's Eve Celebration for a group of friends who called themselves "The Secret Order of Judith." It's perfect for any group of friends who see New Year's Eve as a timely opportunity to celebrate the year past and welcome the new year to come. The evening included happy hours from 7:00 to 9:00 p.m., followed by Part One of the spell from 9:00 to 10:00 p.m., and a feast of a dinner from 10:00 p.m. until shortly before midnight. At midnight, Part Two of the spell took place, followed by dessert, the exchange of gifts, and the pure pleasure of one another's company. The spell ended on the first day of the New Year, shortly before sunrise. All nine members were present.

In addition to everyone contributing food and drink, all were asked to bring three things to the spell: a symbol of something to get rid of from the year past, a symbol of what they wished for the New Year, and gifts for the exchange. Part One took place an hour before dinner. The host prepared a coffee table altar covered with white linen cloth, candles (one for everyone), incense, evergreens and holly, and plenty of room for old and New Year symbols. Taking turns, we each lit a candle, talked about something to let go of in the year past, and placed the symbol on the altar. After all was said and done, the spell moved to the dinner table. Candles were left to burn on the altar, surrounded by symbols of "things be gone." A three-course dinner was served with the holiest of communions, the best of times, wallowing in favorite memories.

Shortly before midnight, Part Two of the spell moved back to the altar, beginning with a champagne toast to the New Year accompanied by rounds of hugs, kisses, and New Year wishes at midnight. Once again, gathered around the altar, over coffee, cordials, and desserts, we took turns making wishes for the New Year. The old year symbols were removed and replaced with New Year symbols, full of heartfelt hope for the year to come. The gift exchange followed, filled with the pleasure of our company, floating in what felt like heaven on earth–as the door to the spirit world opened and we were there. The spell ended when the Judys felt spent, the circle was broken, and everyone departed, shortly before sunrise.

HAPPY NEW YEAR!

BLESSED BE

Rosh Hashanah Blessing

One of the finest features of New York City life is the opportunity to celebrate everyone's holidays and holy days. Rosh Hashanah is the Jewish New Year. This blessing was sent by a Jewish friend, Rabbi Joseph B. Meszler, spiritual leader of Temple Sinai in Sharon, Massachusetts.

On Rosh Hashanah it is written, on Yom Kippur it is sealed:
That this year people will live and die,
some more gently than others
and nothing lives forever.
But amidst overwhelming forces
of nature and humankind,
we still write our own Book of Life,
and our actions are the words in it,
and the stages in our lives are the chapters,
and nothing goes unrecorded, ever.
Every deed counts.
Everything you do matters.
And we never know what act or word
Will leave an impression or tip the scale.
If not now, then when?
For the things we can change, there is t'shuvah, realignment,

For the things we cannot change, there is t'filah, prayer,
For the help we can give, there is tzedakah, justice.
Together, let us write a beautiful Book of Life
for the Holy One to read.

Saint Francis Pet Blessing

If you want to see a Pet Blessing extraordinaire, come to the Cathedral of Saint John the Divine in New York City on the first Sunday in October, near the Feast of Saint Francis of Assisi on October 4. New Yorkers bring cats, dogs, snakes, mice, lizards, birds, fish, hamsters, ferrets, whatever. The folks at Radio City Music Hall bring camels, donkeys, sheep, and ox, all stars in the Christmas Spectacular's Living Nativity. Anyone can have animals blessed at the annual Saint John the Divine Pet Blessing–a glorious experience in New York City's most beautiful cathedral.

If you can't bring your pet to New York City, or if your pet despises group activity, here's a pet blessing you can do at home. While October 4–Feast of Saint Francis–is believed to be the best day for pet blessings, feel free to bless your pets as often as necessary. In case of illness, or just in gratitude for the pure pleasure of their company, a blessing may be called for. This spell is even known to quiet down nonstop barkers and whiners. Never underestimate the power of Saint Francis to bless you and your pets with what you need.

ON THE ALTAR

> pin or knife for carving
> 1 brown candle for each pet

holy water

pet charm (collar, tags, favorite toy)

pet photo

pet treats

THE SPELL

With pet present, carve its name into the candle, anoint with holy water, and light. While holding or petting the animal, pray:

O God, we thank you for
giving us these pets who bring us joy.
As you care for us and all creation,
we ask your help in caring for (or healing) those
who trust us to look after them.
By doing this, we share in your divine love
for all creation.

Then using your right hand, sprinkle holy water on your pet and over the items on the altar. Next, put the collar and tags back on, return the toy, and give your pet treats. Treat yourself too. Let the candles burn until bedtime; then blow them out, rub your hands in the smoke, lay your hands on your pet, and pray *"Blessed Be."*

BLESSED BE

Saint Francis Prayer for Peace

This prayer, known to grant instant peace, is attributed to Saint Francis of Assisi. It's fitting for an opening or closing prayer for healing, get well, and anti-anxiety spells, or easily becomes an instant spell all its own when feeling upset, in need of calming down. Having been prayed and chanted for centuries, this prayer's power to grant peace is miraculous.

> *Make me a channel of your peace,*
> *where there is hatred, let me sow love;*
> *where there is injury, pardon;*
> *where there is doubt, faith;*
> *where there is despair, hope;*
> *where there is darkness, light;*
> *where there is sadness, joy.*
> *O Divine One, grant that I may not so much seek*
> *to be consoled, as to console,*
> *to be understood, as to understand,*
> *to be loved as to love with all my soul.*
> *For it is in giving that we receive,*
> *it is in pardoning that we are pardoned,*
> *it is in dying that we're born to eternal life.*
> *Amen.*

BLESSED BE

True Love Spell

The focus of this spell is granting a wish for true love. It can be used to find a soulmate, revive a relationship, or celebrate true love. If you're wondering whether the love you've found is true, that too can become clear in this spell. Whatever you bring to this spell, have a lovely time. The deities you call upon know the love you seek.

ON THE ALTAR

> red roses
> 6-inch circle of red cloth
> 2 acorns
> 7 rose petals
> small red felt heart
> personal love charms
> pin or knife for carving
> 2 red candles
> anointing oil (rose)
> holy water
> seashells
> 4-inch square white paper
> red ink pen
> gold cord

Place red roses on the altar. Put the red circular cloth in the center of the altar, and all the love charms on top (acorns, rose petals, felt heart, charms). Keep in mind the love charms listed are suggestions. Add yours. This spell begs you to make it your own. The days of the full moon are best for love magic, especially Fridays and Mondays.

DIRECTIONS

1. CANDLE LIGHTING. Before anointing, carve your initials on one red candle, and your true love's initials on the other. If you don't know the initials, carve a heart with a question mark in the center. While anointing, focus on the love you want to draw into your life or the love you are celebrating. While lighting both candles, pray:

O Holy Mother, to you I pray,
come and grant my wish today.
All in true accord with Thee,
as I pray, so might it be,
Grant my wish
(specify wish).
Blessed Be.

Again, feel free to choose your favorite prayer, or let your spirit speak spontaneously. What comes from the heart makes magic. Pause for a moment of silence.

2. BLESSING. Sprinkle holy water on love charms, seashells, and candles. Focus on opening your heart to receive what you wish. If there is someone specific in mind, envision that person as part of your life, present at the altar, standing by your side.

3. SPELL. Take the white paper, and with the red ink pen, draw a heart big enough to write the name or qualities you seek in finding true love. After filling the heart, fold the paper three times, repeating with each fold, *"As I wish, so might it be."* Seal it with a kiss and place it in the center of the red cloth with the other love charms. Tie everything together with the gold cord, using three knots, repeating *"Blessed Be"* after each knot. Leave the love charm on the altar while candles burn. Let it be.

4. CLOSING. When extinguishing the candles, or closing the spell, repeat the "Holy Mother" prayer used in the beginning, or offer a spontaneous prayer in gratitude for your prayer being heard. Place the love charm under your pillow for nine nights–sleep on it–and carry it with you for nine

days. For the next nine evenings, relight the candles and put the love charm on the altar while candles burn, reminding you true love magic is at work. After nine days, scatter rose petals near the love you wish drawn to you. Keep the love charm on the altar, or in a sacred place, for use in repeating true love spells.

BLESSED BE

Saint Anthony Lost and Found Spell

Saint Anthony is the Miracle Saint for finding lost items. The older you get, the more you may need to call on Saint Anthony for help. I could fill a book with testimonies of Saint Anthony's successes with a chapter of my own. This is the prayer to Saint Anthony known to point us in the direction of lost items. My mother swore to its repeated success–particularly with keys–as do I and millions of others. Focus on the lost item being found while repeating seven times:

Dear Saint Anthony,
please come around,
something's lost
and can't be found.

The item will be found within seven days, often sooner. If not, keep repeating and he'll keep looking. What you lost will be found. It will find you.

BLESSED BE

Don't grieve.
Anything you lose comes around
in another form.

−Rumi

Saint Anthony Prayer for a Miracle

In Catholic saint lore, Saint Anthony of Padua, known to find lost items, is also revered as the Saint of Miracles. As with Saint Jude, the hopeless and the desperate are drawn to him. Miracles are the magic of materializing the impossible, making real what we want. In Christian scripture, the blind see, the lame walk, lepers are cured, even the dead rise to new life. In every case, it's belief in miracles that creates the possibility. And here, in this prayer to Saint Anthony, it's our belief in receiving a miracle that grants our prayer. Repeating this prayer every day for nine days is believed to be so powerful that miracles happen. It casts its own spell and grants the miracle we seek.

PRAYER TO SAINT ANTHONY

O Holy Saint Anthony. Gentlest of Saints,
your love for God and God's people
made you worthy, when on earth,
to possess miraculous powers.
Miracles waited on your word,
which you were ever ready to speak
for those in trouble or anxiety.
Encouraged by this thought,

I implore you to obtain for me,
(make your request here).

The answer to my prayer may require a miracle:
even so, you are the Saint of Miracles,
O Gentle and Loving Saint Anthony,
whose heart was ever full of sympathy,
whisper my prayer into the ears of Jesus,
who loved to be folded in your arms,
and the gratitude of my heart will always be yours.
Amen.

BLESSED BE

Blessing at the Hour of Death

A dearly departed friend worked as a hospital chaplain, spending days and nights with the sick and dying, family and friends. This is a blessing she used when the terminally ill were preparing to die. *"What better time for a blessing,"* she wrote, *"than at the hour of death."* I was with her at the hour of her death and found this blessing a perfect parting gift for a best friend.

The divine power in this blessing is twofold, combining anointing rituals of ancient burial rites and the final blessing from the burial rites of nuns. When a sister dies, the community surrounds her, escorts her body to the burial place, and prays for angels to conduct her into paradise. This blessing does the same in providing family and friends an opportunity to anoint their loved one and call on angels to lead them into paradise. There is no more graceful way to help loved ones depart this life than thanking them for the gift of their life and giving them our blessing. Background music is perfect for this blessing, preferably a favorite of the dying. My mother selected three favorites to be played as she departed: Schubert's "Ave Maria," "Amazing Grace" on the bagpipes (just the music, no words), and the soundtrack from *Dirty Dancing*. She nurtured a lifelong crush on Patrick Swayze. At the moment of death, everything is sacred.

ON THE ALTAR

> 2 white candles (if possible, those used in family celebrations)
> anointing oil
> favorite items of the dying

DIRECTIONS

1. CANDLE LIGHTING. Anoint one candle with the dying one's birthday and the other candle with the date of departure. As everyone gathers in a circle around the bed, candles are lit, and a prayer is offered:

> *Holy One, we give back to You*
> *this beloved person (name),*
> *whom you have loaned to us for a short time.*
> *As they have been a blessing to us in this life,*
> *we bless them now for this final journey*
> *to your eternal light and peace.*

2. BLESSING. Everyone present anoints and blesses with a sign of the cross a part of the body with oil (forehead, hands, feet, heart). As this is done, prayers of thanks are offered as each one gives a final blessing. Like all rituals, this one is not to be rushed. This is a time to thank our dying loved one for the life they gave us, sharing favorite memories and funniest stories. Allow time for remembering, laughing,

crying, being silent, singing. We sat around my departing friend Mary eating her favorite dinner–fried chicken, cole-slaw, fries–and sipping her favorite drink, Manhattans. I swabbed her mouth with Manhattans in honor of our Last Supper. Whatever you do, the greatest blessing is giving loved ones a happy death.

3. FINAL BLESSING. As the anointing and blessing ritual draws to a close, all offer together the ancient prayer "In Paradisum":

Saints of God, come to their aid,
come to meet them, Angels of God.
God of mercy, hear our prayer for (name),
whom you have called from this life.
Welcome them into the company of your saints
in the kingdom of light and peace.
Amen.

Play the Gregorian Chant hymn "In Paradisum," or select a closing prayer of your choice. Remember: The most powerful part of any ritual is making it your own.

May they depart this life happily and rest in peace.

BLESSED BE

Sisters' Memorial Blessing

Remembering dearly departed loved ones is something we do naturally, believing as Saint John Chrysostom reveals, *"Those we love and lose are not where they were before; they are now wherever we are."* I believe whenever loved ones come to mind it's because we sense their presence. Spirits communicate through thoughts, dreams, and imagination, ways we understand. So never dismiss thoughts and dreams of loved ones as random, meaningless products of an overactive imagination. Just because it's imagination does not make it any less real. Spirits talk through imagination. One of the most ordinary ways to keep in touch with departed loved ones is to remember them whenever we come together, which happens naturally. This is a blessing of remembrance.

In an enduring ritual of remembrance, my friends, family, and sisters always speak about our departed loved ones, acknowledging their presence whenever we get together. They are wherever we are. As we remember, they become present. At the end of the Annual Assembly of the Sisters for Christian Community, when a litany of names of deceased members is read, everyone there will tell you the room doubles in size as the spirit of every sister steps forward when her name is called. We literally stand on their shoulders. In remembering loved ones and calling them by name, they step forward and become present. Abracadabra and Blessed Be.

This blessing is done whenever loved ones come together, and we make it a point to remember them in spirit. There is nothing strange in remembering departed loved ones whenever we're together. It's completely natural for them to remain with us. In remembering, they become present, transforming sadness over loss into the joy felt through abiding presence. So, whenever you get together with family and friends, light a candle and acknowledge the presence of your dearly departed loved ones. Tell stories about them and their spirits appear. The magic in lasting memories is nothing less than divine in the way loved ones make their presence felt. So whenever you come together, do so in memory of them. See for yourself what extraordinary blessings there are in precious memories and feel for yourself how sadness transforms naturally into its sister joy. The dearly departed are with us wherever we are, and remembrance is our divine connection. This blessing is yours anytime dearly departed come to mind. Light a candle and honor their presence with favorite memories. Call them by name and they appear. Sit with them for a spell and listen. See how sweet it is to be blessed always by the abiding presence of our dearly departed–guardian angels at our side.

BLESSED BE

Love Your Enemy Binding Spell

If someone is making life miserable and you want that person to stop, a binding spell is what you need. For example, a hospital administrator's department was threatened in a takeover by an incompetent individual no one respected. Because that person was a friend of the hospital's president, the unethical move felt all but certain, but the administrator asked for the person to be bound from making the move. We did the binding spell together, and her wish was granted. The incompetent one was removed from consideration, and the administrator got the job with a big promotion. The focus of binding spells is on preventing enemies from hurting you, others, and themselves, as well as protecting everyone concerned from meanness or retribution. Binding spells work for the greatest good of everyone concerned and harm none, including the "enemy." This spell is one of the best ways I know to love the enemy.

ON THE ALTAR

> 3 white candles
> 1 black candle
> 3-inch square white paper
> 1 bay leaf
> pin or knife for carving

anointing oil (eucalyptus is good)

incense burner

black ink pen

Arrange the three white candles in a triangle on the altar with the black candle in the center. Place the white paper square and bay leaf under the black candle.

DIRECTIONS

1. CANDLE LIGHTING. Before anointing the white candles, carve "Holy" into all three; then anoint with oil. Before anointing the black candle, carve the name of the person you want to bind and then anoint. Light only the three white candles when you begin, praying the "Saint Francis Prayer for Peace" (p. 178).

2. INCENSING. Light the incense, allowing smoke to rise. Take the black candle and hold it over the incense, letting the smoke pass over. Do the same with the white paper and bay leaf, praying after each, *"As I wish, so might it be. Blessed be."*

3. SPELL. Light the black candle from the top white one. Hold the lit black candle over the incense, repeating three times, *"I bind you, (name), from doing harm to me, others, and yourself. Blessed be."* Place the black candle back in the center

of the white candle triangle. Take the white paper and pen. Draw a circle of protection on the white paper with your name in the center. Fold it three times, repeating with each fold, *"Blessed be."* Hold the folded paper over the incense; then light it with the flame of the black candle, letting it burn. Take the pen and bay leaf and write on it the name of your enemy. Hold it over the incense, then over the flame of the black candle, repeating once again, *"I bind you* (name) *from doing harm to me, others, and yourself. Blessed be."* Light the bay leaf from the black candle, placing it in the incense burner. Let everything be until bedtime.

4. CLOSING. After extinguishing the candles, repeat the "Saint Francis Prayer for Peace" (p. 178). Leave candle remnants and ashes on the altar for seven days, repeating the "Saint Francis Prayer for Peace" at the end of each day. Within the next thirty days, take the candle remnants and ashes to a river, lake, stream, or ocean and throw them over your left shoulder into the water, repeating once again, *"I bind you* (name) *from doing harm to me, others, and yourself. Blessed be."* It is very important in doing this spell to think only positive thoughts, envisioning your wish being granted, paying no attention to negative thoughts or feelings regarding the bound person. Negative thoughts break

the spell. Remain focused singleheartedly on your wish coming true. Binding spells are best done on Tuesdays and Saturdays, under a new moon.

BLESSED BE

Home Sweet Home Moving Spell

This two-day moving spell is to be done the night before you move and the night after you've moved into a new house or apartment. It can also be adapted for any kind of moving from one place to another (office, retail space, city, etc.). Because everything is packed and you are likely exhausted, everything about this spell is simple and user friendly.

ON THE ALTAR

> pin or knife for carving
> 1 candle
> holy water
> 1 smudge stick/incense
> rock salt

The focus of the first night's spell, the night before you move, is on taking only good energy with you. Carve the old address into the top of the candle, anoint with holy water, and light. Take the incense or smudge stick, light it from the candle, and carry it through the house, allowing its smoke to fill and purify corners, doorways, windows, and around packed boxes. While doing this blessing, be thankful for everything that happened to you there. Then take the rock salt and sprinkle a few grains into the corners of all the rooms. Let the candle burn past where you carved the address and then extinguish, praying, *"Into your hands I commend my spirit. Blessed be."*

The focus of the second night's spell is on purifying the new space of any negative energy left behind from previous residents and then blessing the space to make it sacred. Carve your new address into the bottom of the same candle, anoint with holy water, and light. Just as you did the night before, take the incense or smudge stick throughout the house focusing on all you hope to enjoy in the new space. Take the candle and holy water into every room, sprinkling the same areas that were incensed, blessing every room, praying for the deities and all holy spirits to move in with you. When finished, allow the candle to burn until extinguished, praying in conclusion, *"Into your hands, I commend my spirit. Blessed be."*

After everything is unpacked, sprinkle a few grains of rock salt in the corners of every room, including closets. Rock salt is believed to serve as a psychic purifier and protector in the home. Welcome Home Sweet Home.

BLESSED BE

New Baby Blessing

In this nondenominational baby blessing, newborn life is anointed, blessed, and welcomed by family and friends. It takes place as part of a celebration for the birth of your child, before or after brunch, lunch, or dinner. Parents serve as celebrants, selecting godparents and planning the blessing. While godparents are optional, they come from an ancient tradition of choosing those we want to care for our child as their own. You can call on friends who are rabbis, priests, ministers, or nuns, or you can ask friends to preside over the ritual. Do whatever is most comfortable. Selecting those you want to bless your baby is the first step. Begin preparing one month prior to the blessing date.

ON THE ALTAR

> altar cloth
> altar towel
> statue of Virgin Mary, angel, or goddess
> 1 white candle for each immediate family member
> bell
> anointing oil (in small bowl)
> white wine (in small bowl)
> holy water (in small bowl)
> baby/family treasures

basket of blessings/wishes

blank white cards (business card size)

DIRECTIONS

The mother and godmother prepare the basket of blessings. For everyone present, there is a small white card with a blessing printed on one side and a child's wish on the other side. Think of all the blessings you want your child to have–good health, sense of humor, kindness–and write the word on one side of the card, feeling free to decorate. On the other side of the card, think of the wishes you imagine your child making–toys, books, candy– and do the same, writing the word and decorating the card. Put all the cards in the basket and place on the altar. Family treasures are also placed on the altar.

When the blessing is ready to begin, the mother rings the bell and gathers everyone around the altar. The mother stands in the center holding the child, the father on the left, and the celebrant on her right. The celebrant lights the candles, explains the ritual, and begins the blessing. The celebrant calls on the spirit of departed loved ones to join in blessing the child with their first name, as well as any deity or holy spirit revered by the family. With the altar towel draped over the left arm, the celebrant presents the bowl of oil, inviting the father to anoint and bless the child with the given first name, saying *"I bless you my child with the first name of* (given name)." The celebrant then lays a hand on the child's head, praying for protection throughout life from all violence and harm to body and soul.

The celebrant then calls on the mother to bless the child with a middle name, given in secret by the mother. The celebrant presents the bowl of wine, inviting the mother to anoint the child on the forehead and whisper the middle name secretly. (Being given a secret middle name by the mother is an ancient goddess tradition.) The celebrant lays hands on the child's head, praying the child be blessed with the abiding love of family and friends.

The celebrant presents the bowl of holy water and calls upon the godparents to bless the child with the family name, praying "*I bless you* (name), *with the family name of* (name)." If no godparents are chosen, invite grandparents or other family and friends to bestow this blessing. Both godparents, dipping their hand in holy water and anointing the top of the head, bless the child with the family name. The celebrant lays hands on the child, welcoming the child into the family and into this world.

In closing, the mother invites everyone to bless her child, anointing the child's forehead. The basket of blessings and wishes is passed, everyone draws a card, and one by one, the blessing and wish on the card are revealed. Everyone offers a blessing and wish for the child. After all is said and done, celebrate. Continue to eat, drink, and make merry. Celebrate the joy this child brings to our world.

B LESSED B E

—W ITH GRATITUDE TO E LLEN D OLAN AND A NGELA

The Lord's Prayer

In Christian scripture, this prayer is revealed by Christ as the perfect prayer. As a practicing Jew, Christ addresses this prayer to "Our Father," revering the name of G-d as unspoken–*"hallowed be Thy Name."* He prays we find heaven in all the hell on earth–*"on earth as it is in heaven"*–and that we be given every day *"our daily bread."* We pray to be forgiven as we forgive *"those who trespass against us,"* and to be delivered from the influence of evil. May we find heaven on earth, be given what we need every day, and learn to forgive . . . the perfect prayer.

Our Father,
Who art in heaven,
hallowed be Thy Name.
Thy kingdom come,
Thy will be done,
on earth as it is in heaven
Give us this day our daily bread,
and forgive us our trespasses,
as we forgive those who trespass against us.
For the kingdom, the power, and the glory are Yours,
now and forever.
Amen.

BLESSED BE

Nine Saturdays Fertility Spell

While this fertility spell began with someone trying to become pregnant after multiple unsuccessful attempts, it can be adapted to pray for fertility of all kinds–ideas, work, crops–anything you want to grow into divine life. This ritual focuses on the Virgin Mary, Mother of God, mainly because I grew up with the belief that Mary never turns down a woman's request to give birth. Oddly enough–or not–the women who finally became pregnant with this spell were both Jewish. They also felt a soulful affinity with a deity who is the Mother of God.

Springtime is perfect for fertility spells–especially spring equinox–aligning ourselves with Mother Nature, who wakens new life in the spring. Christians believe that's the time of year–March 25–when the Virgin Mary became pregnant from a visit by an angel. Full moons are perfect for fertility spells, and the Saturday you choose to begin your fertility spell should be spent preparing for a divine visit from an angel.

ON THE ALTAR

    2 white candles
    icon/statue of Virgin Mary
    1 red candle
    pin or knife for carving

oil for anointing

spring flowers

seashells

7 sunflower seeds

incense

cup of wine (or water)

1 egg (raw or boiled)

3 blue candles

DIRECTIONS

1. ANOINTING. Place the two white candles on either side of the Virgin and the red one in front. Carve your birth date on one white candle and your partner's birth date on the other white candle. On the other candle, carve the date of birth should you conceive now. Anoint all three candles, focusing on the divine intervention about to occur. Place the flowers, sunflower seeds, and shells on the altar as well.

2. INCENSING. Light the incense, holding the cup of wine over its smoke, praying with your partner, *"As we wish, so might it be. Blessed be."* Pass the incense over all the items on the altar; then incense each other, praying *"As we wish, so might it be. Blessed be."*

3. CANDLE LIGHTING. Light the candle signifying the mother, praying:

Holy Mother, to You we pray,
come and grant our wish today,
all in true accord with Thee,
as we pray, so might it be,
Bless us with a child,
Blessed be.

Light the candle signifying the partner and repeat the prayer. Light the candle signifying the child and repeat the prayer. After the candle lighting, the couple shares the cup of wine, seals the spell with the Holy Kiss, signaling the moment divine intervention has begun.

4. CLOSING. Let the candles burn until bedtime. Before extinguishing, pray together the "Memorare" (p. 128). Within seven days, take the spell remnants–candle stubs, ashes, seeds–to a river at sunset, toss them into the water, praying *"Blessed be."* Then every Saturday for the next seven Saturdays, burn a candle in front of the Virgin Mary and pray the "Memorare." Whenever you are at home during the nine weeks of this spell, keep a candle burning in front of the Virgin Mary, signaling her abiding presence to you,

reminding you the magic of her divine intervention is at work.

THE NINTH SATURDAY SPELL

On the ninth Saturday, repeat the spell done in the beginning. To the altar, add one egg and three blue candles. The focus of the ninth Saturday is on thanksgiving, good health, and all obstacles being removed to conception and birth. Drawing on the power in repetition, repeat your Ninth Saturday Spell at the same time as the first, repeating every gesture, including taking the remnants to a river in seven days. A personal gesture of thanks is important at this time, given that your wish has already been granted. Giving thanks in advance intensifies the magic at work, as does praying the "Memorare" nightly. Then let it be.

Change the spell to make it your own. While this spell worked divinely for two women I know, what you do personally with this spell will work just as well. The more personal the ritual, the more fully charged it is with magic.

BLESSED BE

Friday Night Lights: Shabbat

On Friday nights, Jews all over the world celebrate the ancient tradition of Shabbat with the lighting of candles, welcoming a day of rest at the end of the work week. They keep holy the Sabbath. According to Jewish law, Shabbat is observed a few minutes before sunset on Friday evening, until the appearance of three stars in the sky on Saturday night. Shabbat is revered as a day of rest, so necessary to the soul of humanity it was made a commandment. We need to set aside one day a week from work, devoted to rest and spiritual enrichment. Leisure. Play. With five plus days of work life, the soul begs for one day to rest, one day devoted to spiritual life and the life of the family. Humanity needs at least one day a week for soul food.

At the beginning of Shabbat, the woman of the house presides. The home is her synagogue. At least eighteen minutes before sunset, she lights two candles, passes her hands over the candles a few times, and then covers her eyes with her hands and prays this blessing:

Blessed are you, Lord our G-d, sovereign of the universe,
Who has sanctified us with His commandments
and commanded us
to light the lights of Shabbat.

After the blessing is complete, she uncovers her eyes, and, in the words of a friend, "looks at the lit candles as if for the first time." Some families light more candles, in accord with the number of children, and sometimes each woman and girl lights her own candle. Occasionally, two songs are sung: one greeting two Shabbat angels into the house, and the other praising the woman of the house for all the work she does. The blessing continues over dinner and carries through until three stars appear on Saturday night.

In a spirit of union with Jews all over the world, we are all called to keep holy the Sabbath, giving ourselves a day of rest, a day to take care of our soul and the soul of our family. At sunset on Fridays, light two candles, welcome angels into your home, be thankful for the woman of the house, and enjoy a meal together, the Holiest Communion.

Shalom Shabbat.

BLESSED BE

Saint Therese Email Blessing

While I am no fan of email prayer chains and haven't died (yet) from not forwarding to ten others, this prayer to Saint Therese of Lisieux has a reputation of granting wishes, and I can attest to the fact she's granted me quite a few. The email specified sending this prayer to four others, then watching what happens on the fourth day. I didn't send it to four others, but I did bless four others with my prayer for them, and on the fourth day, all five of us received great surprises. So, make a wish before offering this prayer to Saint Therese–believed to be very powerful– and watch what happens in four days. Email it to four others or pray this prayer for four others. May all of you receive great surprises on the fourth day.

MAKE A WISH

May there be peace within today.
May you trust your highest power
that you are exactly where you are meant to be.
May you not forget the infinite possibilities
that are born of faith.
May you use those gifts that you have received,
and pass on the love that has been given to you.
May you be content knowing you are a child of God.

Let this presence settle into our bones,
and all our souls the freedom to sing,
dance, and bask in the sun...
it is there for each and every one of you.

BLESSED BE

Spell to Become a Peacemaker

Every morning I light a candle and renew my vow to make peace on earth, praying to become a blessing. This spell is that simple. Peacemakers are blessed as true people of God, and becoming a peacemaker is one vow I believe we're all called to profess. Vows are sacred promises, intended to be made and renewed in order to transform us into what we promise. For example, as sisters, we promise to live simply in vowing poverty, we promise to live a solitary life in vowing celibacy, and in vowing obedience we promise to listen to the voice of God speaking in one another when making decisions. We live by consensus. In renewing those vows year after year, they become us. We become what we promise. Our lives become transformed in ways leading us to love the solitary life, to love living simply, and to cherish discerning the truth by listening to God speak in one another.

Taking a vow to become a peacemaker is the purpose of this spell. Stand before the altar. Light a candle. Pause for a moment of silence to focus your attention on the flame, on the presence of God, and join all of us who have taken the *Pax Christi Vow of Non-Violence.*

I vow to carry out in my life the love of Christ:
By striving for peace within myself
and seeking to be a peacemaker in my daily life.

By accepting suffering in the struggle for justice
rather than inflicting it.
By refusing to retaliate
in the face of provocation and violence.
By living conscientiously and simply
so I do not deprive others of the means to live.
By working nonviolently to abolish war,
and the causes of war from my own heart
and from the face of the earth.
Amen.
May the Peace of Christ prevail on earth.

BLESSED BE

Veni Creator Spiritu

"Come Creator Spirit" is a prayer that monks, nuns, priests, and the universal Catholic Church have been praying and chanting for centuries. Calling on the Creator Spirit is perfect for solving problems of all kinds, also invaluable to those working in the arts. Inspiration, insight, and new ideas are all gifts of the Holy Spirit, as are knowledge, wisdom, understanding, counsel, and the strength to do what's right. This is the prayer inviting the Holy Spirit to come into our life and grant our prayer. The feast of the Holy Spirit is Pentecost Sunday, the fiftieth day after Easter, birthday of Christianity. Whenever you feel the need for insight, understanding, or inspiration, light a candle, and pray for the Creator Spirit to come. You can also pause for moments of silence and listen to the Gregorian Chant *Veni Creator Spiritu.*

Come, O Creator, Spirit blest,
In our souls take up your rest.
Come with your grace and heavenly aid,
To fill the hearts which you have made.
O Comforter, to you we cry,
O Heavenly gift of God Most High,
O fount of life and fire of love,
And sweet anointing from above.

You in your sevenfold gifts are known,
You, finger of God's hand we own;
You promise of the Father, You,
Who do the tongue with power imbue.
Kindle our senses from above,
Make our hearts overflow with love.
With patience firm and virtue high,
The weakness of our flesh supply.
Far from us drive the foe we dread,
Grant us your true peace instead.
So shall we not, with You for guide,
Turn from the path of life aside.
Oh, may your grace on us bestow,
The Father and the Son to know.
And You, through endless times confessed,
Of both the eternal spirit blessed.
Now to the Father and the Son,
Who rose from death, be glory given,
With You O Holy Comforter
Henceforth by all in earth and heaven.
Amen.

BLESSED BE

Akta Lakota Great Spirit Prayer

In praying for the blessing of Holy Spirit, the Great Spirit Prayer of an unknown Akta Lakota Indian is also charged powerfully with the prayerful energy of countless generations. Tapping into the prayers of religious traditions connects us in spirit, with our name added to the litany of those who have prayed those words before us. Because Native American prayers are profoundly reflected in the divine power of nature, this prayer calls us to be surrounded by nature where we can hear more clearly the voice of the Great Spirit speak in the wind, the sunset, in every leaf and rock. Find a quiet place outside, wrap yourself in solitude, and let your soul pray the Great Spirit Prayer.

O Great Spirit, whose voice I hear in the wind,
Whose breath gives life to all the world, hear me.
I need your strength and wisdom.
Let me walk in beauty,
and make my eyes ever behold the red and purple sunset.
Make my hands respect the things you have made,
and my ears sharp to hear your voice.
Make me so wise that I may understand
the truths you have taught my people.
Help me remain calm and strong
in the face of all that comes toward me.

Let me learn the lessons you have hidden
in every leaf and rock.
Help me seek pure thoughts free from selfishness
so I may act with the intention of helping others.
Help me find compassion
without empathy overwhelming me.
I seek strength not to feel greater than my brother.
Make me always ready to come to you with clean hands and
   clear eyes,
So when life fades, as the fading sunset,
my spirit may come to you with a pure heart.

BLESSED BE

Two-Day Purification Spell

Purification spells are done to transform awful effects of terrible experiences and prepare us for new sources of life, sure to come. When the worst of times is all we know, it's difficult not to wallow in the worst of feelings. Anger, depression, resentment, confusion, judgment, a desire for payback–all torment with such a powerful force of negativity it becomes nearly impossible to feel any other way. Purification spells work to neutralize negative energy, transforming awful feelings into sources of feeling better. The magic here shifts attention to counting blessings and focusing on new life rising from what feels dead and gone; it grants us peace. The more terrible the experience, the more powerful transformation is at work in our life, and nothing kickstarts the miracle of transformation more effectively than purification spells, best done under a new moon.

ON THE ALTAR

1 red candle
pin or knife for carving
anointing oil
fresh flowers
new life symbol or charm
incense

two 3-inch squares of white paper
red ink pen
small glass bowl
1 white candle

DIRECTIONS

DAY ONE: NEW MOON

1. CANDLE LIGHTING. On day one, use the red candle. Before anointing, carve into the candle a symbol or word of what you want removed from your life. While anointing, focus on opening the soul's door for misery to leave. Place the candle in the center of the altar, with fresh flowers, putting purification charms on top of white paper squares. Light the candle.

Pause for a moment of silence, acknowledging the presence of deities, and pray the Cheyenne Prayer of Peace.

Let me know peace.
For as long as the moon shall rise.
For as long as the rivers shall flow,
For as long as the sun shall shine,
For as long as the grass shall grow,
Let me know peace.

2. INCENSING. In purification spells, we purify and incense the home as well as the items on the altar. Carry the incense through the living space, allowing its smoke to pass over and purify everything of negative energy. While incensing, focus specifically on what you want removed from your life. One woman I know sang "I'm Gonna Wash That Man Right Out of My Hair," while incensing, and it worked. After purifying the space, return to the altar. Hold the red candle and white squares of paper over the incense, praying:

    O Holy Mother, to you I pray,
    Come and grant my prayer today,
    All in true accord with Thee,
    As I pray so might it me,
    Grant my prayer
    (specify wish).
    Blessed Be.

3. SPELL. Take one square of white paper, and in red ink, draw a circle and write within what you want removed from your life (fear, anger, depression, etc.). Read the items aloud, praying after each, *"Be gone. Blessed be."* Place the paper under the burning candle. Let it be.

4. CLOSING. When extinguishing the candle, pray, *"Into your hands, I commend my spirit. Blessed be."* Reserve incense ashes and candle stub.

DAY TWO: NIGHT AFTER NEW MOON

On the following night, repeat the spell at the same time, if possible. The focus of the second night is on what you want to bring into your life, what you hope to happen. Carve into the white candle your birth date and a symbol of your hope. On the second square of white paper, draw a circle in red ink, writing within what you want to happen now, your heart's desire. Everything else remains the same. Repeat the spell.

Before the next new moon (thirty days), take the incense ashes, candle stubs, and white paper to a river, toss over your left shoulder into the water, pray, *"Blessed Be,"* walk away, and don't look back. You will feel better. You will be granted peace.

BLESSED BE

Our Lady of Lourdes Get Well Blessing

So powerful is faith in Our Lady of Lourdes that thousands of healing miracles are attributed to her divine intervention. Even today, thousands more travel to Lourdes, France, believing they too will be cured at the site she appeared on February 11, 1858, to a young girl, Bernadette Soubirous, and her two sisters. Bathing in the spring at the shrine or drinking the water is believed to have healing powers, as does the "Prayer to Our Lady of Lourdes," bearing the prayerful energy of all the sick and cured. The act of repeating this prayer and blessing yourself with holy water is believed to be full of healing power; the next best thing to being there.

> *O ever Immaculate Virgin, Mother of Mercy,*
> *health of the sick, refuge of sinners,*
> *comforter of the afflicted,*
> *you know my wants, my troubles, my sufferings;*
> *look with mercy on me.*
> *By appearing in the Grotto at Lourdes,*
> *you were pleased to make it a privileged sanctuary,*
> *where you grant your favors.*
> *Already many sufferers have obtained*
> *the cure of their infirmities,*
> *body and soul.*

I come, therefore, with complete confidence
to implore your maternal intercession.
Obtain, O Loving Mother, the grant of my request,
(make request here).
Through gratitude for your favors,
I endeavor to imitate your virtues,
that I may one day share your glory.
Amen.

Bless yourself with holy water and let it be.

BLESSED BE

Three-Day Success Spell

Success spells are for those who wish to excel at the work and life they love. This has nothing to do with luck, but everything to do with the cycle of life and coming into our own–fulfilling what we are meant to do in this lifetime. When we put all our energy into work we love, the magic of success is always at work. This spell taps into the magic of work we love, blessing us with the success we envision, the success of which often feels beyond control. Recognizing success is a gift of the deities, this spell is God's blessing on a work well done and a life well lived. Success spells are best done on Sundays, under a full moon.

ON THE ALTAR

    pin or knife for carving
    3 purple candles
    anointing oil
    4 white candle
    3-inch square white paper
    incense
    symbol of success wish
    7 rose petals
    green ink pen

1. CANDLE LIGHTING. Carve the word "Holy" into the three purple candles, arranging in a triangle on the altar. On the white candle, carve your initials and a word or symbol of the success you seek. Place the white candle in the center of the triangle, on top of the paper square. While anointing, focus on all obstacles to success being removed. Light the three purple candles, praying after each.

Holy Mother, to You I pray,
Come and grant my prayer today.
All in true accord with Thee,
As I pray, so might it be,
Grant my wish,
(make your wish).
Blessed be.
Pause for a moment of silence.

2. INCENSING. Light incense from the top purple candle, allowing smoke to rise. Hold the white candle over the incense, passing it through the smoke, focusing on your wish coming true. Light the white candle from the flame of the top purple candle, placing it back in the center of the triangle, on top of the white paper. Take the symbol of your

success (business card, manuscript, resume, etc.), pass it through the smoke of the incense, hold it over the flame of the white candle, repeating the "Holy Mother" prayer.

3. SPELL. Take the paper from under the white candle, and with the green pen, draw a circle. Within the circle, write the word carved into the white candle. Fold the paper three times, seal with a kiss, praying with each fold, *"As I wish, so might it be. Blessed be."* Light the paper from the white candle, allowing it to burn with the incense, or in a small metal bowl, repeating again the "Holy Mother" prayer.

4. CLOSING. Before bedtime, extinguish the candles, praying *"Blessed be"* after each is snuffed out. For extra power, repeat this spell for three nights under a full moon. Reserve the remains (ashes, candle stubs, etc.) on the altar. Sprinkle in a garden or flower pot within thirty days. Let it be.

BLESSED BE

Monthly Retreat Spell

Retreating for a day at the beginning of every month is a revered tradition in the sisterhood, one I wish the whole world revered. When I was a young nun, all days felt like retreat days, wrapped in solitude, full of silence and scheduled prayers. The first Sunday of every month, Retreat Sunday, only felt different because we got to sleep a little later and had more unscheduled time. Eventually (and over fifty years later) the first Sunday of every month turned into my favorite day of the month, retaining the feeling of a retreat day. No work, only play. An "Anything Can Happen Day," full of nothing other than reading, letter writing, painting, maybe a film festival, doing whatever I feel called to do next, always a spell. The focus of this spell–done at the beginning and end of the day–is on blessing the best and worst times of the month past and becoming soulfully receptive to the best and hardest times in the month to come. Everything comes with a purpose, a message, and at the beginning of the month, this spell opens us to see more clearly the purpose in whatever happens in the month to come. In this spell we pray to accept everything as holy, just as it is.

ON THE ALTAR

> symbol of the best part of the month
>
> symbol of the worst part of the month
>
> 2 white candles
>
> 3-inch square white paper
>
> flowers
>
> pin or knife for carving
>
> anointing oil
>
> incense
>
> small metal bowl or incense burner

Assemble the items on the altar, placing the best and worst symbols in the center with a candle on each side.

DIRECTIONS

1. CANDLE LIGHTING. Before anointing, carve the month past into one candle and the new month into the other. While anointing, focus on the best and worst of the past month, praying to see the message given. Light the candles, praying "*Veni Creator Spiritu*" (p. 243), or your own prayer invoking the Holy Spirit to enlighten you, enabling you to see more clearly the holiness in everything to come. Pause for a moment of silence, acknowledging the presence of God.

2. INCENSING. Light the incense, allowing its smoke to rise. Hold the lit candle on the left–symbolizing the month past–over the incense, focusing on blessing and purifying the best and worst of the month, praying, *"Blessed be."* Then hold the candle on the right over the incense, praying for a blessing on the month to come and the grace to accept everything as holy, just as it is, repeating, *"Blessed be."*

3. SPELL. Let the candles and incense burn through the day, keeping the door to the spirit world open, making the retreat day holy. The whole day becomes a spell, full of divine activity, an "anything can happen day" full of whatever you want. If you keep a daily journal, as I do, it becomes a perfect time to read through the past month and see more clearly what happened. Identify the best part of the month and write it in a circle on one side of the 3-inch square paper. Identify the hardest part of the month and write it in a circle on the other side of the paper. Find a symbol of both and place on top of the paper in the center of the altar between the candles. Let it be.

4. CLOSING. Shortly before the end of the day, fold the paper three times, repeating *"Blessed be"* with each fold, sealing with a kiss. Light the paper from the flame of the

candle on the right–representing the month to come–and let it burn in the censor or metal dish. While it burns, offer a prayer of thanksgiving for the month past and the month to come. In extinguishing the candles, pray, *"Into your hands, I commend my spirit. Blessed be."* Day is done. The following morning, sprinkle the ashes in a garden or flowerpot.

BLESSED BE

I will lead you into the desert,
and speak to your heart.

Happy Anniversary Blessing

Any anniversary–birth, death, marriage, divorce, hiring, firing–
is a powerful day, charged with life-changing energy. Something
happened on that day, making it one of the most important
days of our life. In retrospect, those days can be seen as full of
divine activity, a gift of the deities. This ritual can be done to
remember and celebrate any anniversary. Because anniversaries
are profoundly personal, it's up to you to improvise for special
occasions. The focus of all anniversary rituals is on connecting
to the divine energy, the magic moment that turned an ordinary
day into an anniversary. We return to the memory of that day,
reflect on how that day changed our life, and pray in gratitude
for transforming turning points, the joyful and sorrowful mysteries of our life.

All anniversaries are holy days, so if possible, take the day off
from work to celebrate, to remember and honor the day as holy.
Create an anniversary altar, placing symbols of the occasion you're
celebrating in the center, surrounded by candles. For example,
when I celebrate the anniversary of my friend Molly's departure
from this life–November 2–I place her photo on the altar along
with a pack of unfiltered Camel cigarettes–her drug of choice–and
items she made, charged with her energy. It's a day to wallow in
all the precious memories marking that day as an anniversary. In
the morning, offer thanks for the anniversary given that day and

prepare to receive surprising blessings the day promises. At night, celebrate and be grateful for blessings received.

This is a day of your making, a day to create your own spell and blessing. Light candles. Burn incense. Call to mind magic anniversary-making moments–the best of times–and make wishes. Offer thanks for the anniversary you celebrate and the ways in which your life is blessed. Anniversaries are holy days in our lives, begging to be remembered, full of divine energy capable of transforming our life every time we celebrate the memory. Make it an important part of your life to celebrate all the anniversaries you've been given. Each one is a source of endless blessings, full of grace.

BLESSED BE

Get Well Spell

This spell can be done for yourself or someone else, focusing on removing disease and discomfort from mind, body, and soul, restoring good health and well-being. The magic in this spell works in freeing us to feel good. It asks whatever sickens and causes pain to leave us, summoning healing energy to feel better, to get well. In doing this spell, focus on feeling good, not on the cause of sickness. Let sick feelings be, paying no attention. In praying sickness to leave, welcome feeling good, believing our prayer is being granted in the working of this spell. While any day is a good day for a "Get Well Spell," Tuesdays and Thursdays are believed to be more powerful than others.

ON THE ALTAR

6-inch square of green cloth

1 blue candle

1 green candle

angel figure/symbol (small)

7 eucalyptus leaves

crystal or sacred stone

personal healing charm

blue cord

3-inch square white paper

pin or knife for carving

anointing oil

holy water/branch for blessing

green ink pen

photo of the person in need of healing

Put green cloth in the center of the altar, placing the blue candle on the left and green candle on the right. In the center of the green cloth, put the angel, eucalyptus leaves, crystal or stone, healing charm, blue cord, and white paper.

DIRECTIONS

1. CANDLE LIGHTING. Before anointing, carve into the blue candle a word or symbol of what you want healed (pain, cancer, fear, etc.), and into the green candle what you wish for and initials of the sick person. While anointing, focus on healing energy pouring into the one in need. Light both candles, extend your hands over the flames, pause for a moment of silence, acknowledge the presence of deities, and pray for a blessing. The "Our Lady of Lourdes Get Well Blessing" (p. 224) and the "Prayer to Saint Jude" (p. 144) are fitting here, as is personal prayer.

2. BLESSING. Sprinkle and bless with holy water all the items on the altar, yourself, and anyone else present. If you

have pets, it's good to have them present. Pets are known to bear healing power. While blessing with holy water, focus on the life-giving power in water to restore life and well-being, praying the one in need receives its healing blessing.

3. SPELL. Take the white paper, and with the green ink pen, write the specific health request. Fold the paper three times, repeating after each fold, *"As I wish, so might it be."* Seal with a kiss. Then gather all the items in the green cloth and tie together with blue cord using three knots, praying after each, *"Blessed be."* Leave the charm on the altar between the candles. Let it be.

4. CLOSING. Before bedtime, extinguish each candle, praying, *"Into your hands I commend my spirit. Blessed be."* Place the "get well" charm under your pillow for nine nights, conscious of healing magic at work. Carry it with you, wherever you go, for nine days. If you're doing the spell for others, give them the charm and have them do the same. Or, if they don't live near, place the charm on their photo and leave it on the altar, lighting a candle there every day. After nine days, unwrap the charm, bury the folded paper in a garden or flower pot, and scatter the eucalyptus near an evergreen tree, or another healing place. Keep the other healing charms

on the altar, or in a sacred place for future use, reminding you of your power to make healing magic.

BLESSED BE

Healing Bedside Blessing

The laying on of hands is an ancient ritual believed to have healing powers. In Christian scripture, Christ heals and performs miracles with the laying on of hands. This simple blessing can be done whenever two or three gather around the sick. In the sisterhood it's an ordinary blessing, as it is among all those who believe healing comes through the laying on of hands and praying together over the one in need of healing. While any of the prayers in this book are fitting here, there are no prayers more powerful than those spoken by the ones whose hands lay on the sick. When you pray in that way, the power in your hands is charged with healing energy, your touch divine. If you want to heal your sick body and soul, or that of friends and loved ones, lay a hand upon the sore spot, lay your other hand upon the sick, and let your soul pray for a healing blessing. You, and those gathered with you, will be granted peace. Something in you will be healed.

BLESSED BE

Good Luck Spell

Good luck is not something we get whenever we want, feeling beyond control. Some have it and some don't. Some appear luckier than others, like those who win the lottery multiple times. Even so, I believe there's a lot more to luck than meets the eye, making it infinitely more than a random blessing. I also believe there is no such thing as coincidence, meaning we can align ourselves with the forces of good luck, putting us in the right place at the right time, where the magic of good luck happens. This spell opens the possibility of conditions being made right, of everything being lined up perfectly for good luck to enter our life. So if you have done everything you can to make something happen, and all you need is a bit of luck, this spell opens the door of luck to help make your wish come true. Try this spell and see for yourself how calling on deities for divine intervention helps good luck appear where most needed.

ON THE ALTAR

- 1 flowering plant (a violet, if possible)
- 1 purple candle
- good luck charms
- 5-inch purple circular cloth
- gold cord
- anointing oil (violet scented)

incense

holy water

pin or knife for carving

Place the items on the altar, putting the flowering plant behind the purple candle. Violets are believed to have special powers to attract good luck. Surround the plant with good luck charms.

DIRECTIONS

4. CANDLE LIGHTING. Before anointing, carve into the candle a good luck symbol, your initials, and your birth date. Anoint with oil, focusing on allowing yourself to be in the right place at the right time. Light the candle, pause for a moment of silence, focus on your wish, and offer a prayer acknowledging the presence of deities and asking for divine intervention. Offer a personal prayer or the "Holy Mother" prayer.

Holy Mother, to you I pray,
come and grant my wish today,
all in true accord with Thee,
as I pray, so might it be,
grant my luck wish,
(specify wish).
Blessed Be.

2. INCENSING. Light the incense, passing its smoke over the items on the altar, focusing on all obstacles being removed to good luck coming your way. Allow the incense to purify your thoughts of any doubt or disbelief in the power of luck to enter your life.

3. SPELL. Make your lucky charm. First, sprinkle the items with holy water, repeating, *"As I wish, so might it be."* Gather everything together in the purple cloth, tie in three knots with gold cord, repeating after each knot, *"Blessed Be."*

4. CLOSING. Extinguish the candle, praying, *"Into your hands, I commend my Spirit. Blessed Be."* Place the good luck charm under your pillow at night. Sleep on it. Carry it with you when you leave the house, believing in its power to put you in the right place at the right time. At all other times, leave it on the altar, reminding you of its power, and yours, to bring good luck into your life or the lives of those for whom you pray. Good Luck.

BLESSED BE

Guardian Angel Protection Blessing

There is an ancient belief about everyone being given an angel who prepared our soul for the human experience, remained with us at the moment of birth, and stays with us throughout life, guiding and protecting. In Catholic grade school, we were reminded daily of the presence of our guardian angels, being asked to scoot over at our desks to make room for them to sit beside us. Even those who are not religious believe in angels, having had experiences of inexplicable divine intervention, protecting them from harm, even saving their life in death-defying accidents. I've heard countless stories of angelic intervention being the only explanation for what otherwise would have been a deadly accident. Being surrounded constantly by angelic spirits is a divine comfort in this life, especially with children being told at bedtime to sleep tight *"and don't let the bedbugs bite."* I also sleep with feet outside the covers, counting on my angel to protect me from anyone under the bed reaching up to grab my ankles when the lights go out.

Growing up conscious of an angel at my side leads me to feel very well protected on the streets of New York City, where being struck by car, bus, or taxi is not unlikely. Twice I have been "brushed" by speeding cars, when a split second forward made all the difference in my world. In a car accident during a blizzard some years ago, the car was totaled, but I walked away with only a fractured collar bone. I cultivate daily contact with my angel, remembering the prayer we learned as children, continuing to pray before walking out the door. This blessing encourages us to acknowledge the presence of angels in our life, praying daily for their guidance and protection.

Angel of God,
my guardian dear,
to whom God's love,
commits me here.
Ever this day (night)
be at my side,
to light,
to guard,
to love,
and to guide,
Amen.

For as long as this prayer has been prayed by children (and adults), it carries a powerful blessing. Put angels on your altar, along with photos of dearly departed loved ones–angels in our life–keeping in mind their protective presence above us, below us, beside us, and within us. Angels are messengers of God. At the beginning or ending of every day, light a candle and listen. Our angels are waiting to enlighten, to guard, to love, and to guide. Amen.

BLESSED BE

Days of the Dead Spell

The Days of the Dead are October 31, November 1, and November 2–All Hallows' Eve, All Saints Day, and All Souls Day. We begin to celebrate the Days of the Dead with Halloween on October 31–Wiccan New Year–when the veil between seen and unseen, this world and the spirit world, lifts completely and dearly departed loved ones visit three days. Because the door between worlds is wide open, our lives become charged with divinely enchanted energy, making these days full of grace. The magic begins with envisioning loved ones stopping by for a spell, partying under the full harvest moon for three days. October 31 is their arrival date. It's then we're called to acknowledge their presence, honor and remember them, and pray for the blessing given in the pure pleasure of their company. Light candles in front of their photos. Welcome them home for a spell.

November 1 is All Saints Day, remembering all saints we know, the second Day of the Dead. In thinking about what to do on this day, I always think of those in New Orleans and Mexico who understand the dead more soulfully and insightfully than any other place on earth. Today's the perfect day to tap into the energy of billions who thrive on the ancient tradition of making ancestor altars. On your altar put photos of saints and departed loved ones, items that belonged to them, even their favorite food and drink. I always put out Camel cigarettes (without filter) for my friend Molly, a bottle of whiskey for Dad, and donuts for Mom. Anoint a white candle, calling all your saints to bless you with their presence. When you light the candle, they step forward and join you. Blessed be.

November 2 is celebrated as All Souls Day, the day we honor all departed souls, especially our loved ones. It's also last of the Days of the Dead when the veil between worlds begins to close and our spirit visitors return home. Keep candles burning. Take time alone to sit and listen for messages. We see and hear more clearly these days. Talk to your dearly departed and they will answer. Talk to them every day and you will know they are wherever you are. In whatever way you remember the dead in your life, doing so on these three days is extra powerful. The veil is lifted. Trick and treat yourself by celebrating the Days of the Dead every year. Let yourself be blessed by the loving presence of your dearly departed, along with all visiting angels and saints. Acknowledging–and honoring–their presence is as full of fun as it is in blessings. See for yourself how alive our dearly departed really are. Boo.

BLESSED BE

Prayer for Comfort

The Psalms are some of the most soulful prayers we know, effecting what they signify, which is to say they see in nature the story of life. Psalm 23, the Shepherd Psalm, is powerful in granting comfort. I must have had a past life as a shepherd, because my connection to shepherd images is inexplicably strong, and this psalm is a favorite for as long as I can remember. Whenever you feel in need of comfort, put yourself in a solitary place, light a candle, pause for a moment of silence, and pray this psalm. The divine energy of everyone who has prayed this psalm will comfort you. You stand on their shoulders.

PSALM 23

> *The Lord is my shepherd,*
> *I need nothing more.*
> *You give me rest in green meadows,*
> *setting me near calm waters,*
> *where you revive my spirit.*
> *You guide me along sure paths,*
> *You are true to your name.*
> *Though I should walk in death's dark valley,*
> *I fear no evil with you by my side,*
> *Your shepherd's staff to comfort me.*

You spread a table before me
as my foes look on.
You sooth my head with oil;
My cup is more than full.
Goodness and love will tend me
Every day of my life,
I will dwell in the house of God
As long as I shall live.
Amen.

BLESSED BE

Anxiety Be Gone Spell

Few things in life are worse than the feelings of dread and fear. Both prevent us from being able to find heaven in all the hell on earth, paralyzing us with anxiety and misery. This spell gets rid of everything we dread and fear, removing all sources of anxiety. The focus is on anxiety being gone, feeling better, doing only things that feel good, putting energy in work we love. We open the door to feeling better and walk in. This spell begs you to make it your own. In making it my own, this is what I did.

ON THE ALTAR

> 5-inch circle of blue cloth
> 2 blue candles
> fresh flowers
> angel medal
> pin or knife for carving
> anointing oil
> incense
> 3-inch square white paper
> blue ink pen
> bay leaf
> rock salt
> holy water
> gold cord

Place the angel medal, bay leaf, rock salt, and anything else you want on the blue cloth in the center of the altar, with a blue candle on each side.

DIRECTIONS

1. CANDLE LIGHTING. Before anointing, carve into the candles a symbol of what you dread or fear. Anoint the candles, focusing on how it would feel to live without dread and fear. Rub good energy into the carved symbols. Then light the candles and pause for a moment of silence, acknowledging the presence of the deities. Welcome deities with a personal prayer, or the "Saint Francis Prayer for Peace" (p. 178), "Prayer for Comfort" (p. 246), and "Saint Jude Blessing for the Impossible" (p. 144).

2. INCENSING. Light the incense, passing its smoke over the items on the altar. Hold each candle over the smoke, praying, *"Be gone. Blessed be."* While incensing, envision all fear and anxiety leaving your life. Let it go. Let it go. Let it go.

3. SPELL. Take the white paper and draw a circle in the center with a blue ink pen. Within the circle, write what you dread and fear most. Fold the paper three times, repeating after each fold, *"Be gone. Blessed be."* Seal it with a kiss. Kiss it good-bye. Put the paper in the blue cloth, cover it

with the bay leaf, and then sprinkle with rock salt and holy water. Gather everything together in the blue cloth, making a charm bag, and with gold cord, tie seven knots, repeating after each, *"Blessed be."*

4. CLOSING. When extinguishing candles, repeat one of the prayers used in the beginning, or offer personal prayer. Place the charm bag under your pillow for nine days and nights. Before the next new moon, take the charm bag to the water, toss over your left shoulder, and don't look back. If you're not near water, bury in a garden or flowerpot. Let it go.

Peace be with you.

BLESSED BE

An Irish Blessing

May the blessing of light be with you–
light outside and light within.
May sunlight shine upon you and warm your heart,
'til it glows like a great peat fire
so that strangers may come and warm themselves by it.
May a blessed light shine out of your two eyes
like a candle set in two windows of a house,
bidding the wanderer to come in out of the storm.
May you ever give a kindly greeting to those
whom you pass as you go along the roads.
May the blessing of rain
–the sweet soft rain–
fall upon you
so that little flowers may spring up
to shed their sweetness in the air.
May the blessings of the earth
–the good, rich earth–
be with you.
May earth be soft under you when you rest upon it,
tired at the end of day.
May earth rest easy over you when at last you lie under it,

May the earth rest so lightly over you
that your spirit may be out from it quickly,
and up, and off, and on its way back to God.

BLESSED BE

A Closer Walk with Thee

Walking every day can become a soul-saving ritual. This is a blessing on yourself. Whether it's walking outside or journeying into the soul, we need to give ourselves one hour a day for a "closer walk with Thee." We need one hour every day to wrap ourselves in solitary splendor and let our spirit roam. In the care and feeding of the soul, walking is known for its mysterious power in solving problems and conveying messages from angels, including new ideas for creative projects.

If your days are too full for one hour a day, start with less and you'll want to work up to more. You have to take the time for yourself because no one will give it to you (unless you become a nun). So, bless yourself every day in a "closer walk with Thee." Go outside for a walk, go inside for a walk, follow your spirits wherever they roam. Our souls need to be blessed in this way. Out of twenty-four hours, taking one for the care and feeding of the soul is not a big ask. It's daily bread. Welcome the ritual of walking into your life and see what a difference it makes in your world. Bless yourself every day in a "closer walk with Thee."

BLESSED BE

Thanksgiving Spells and Blessings

In closing, being grateful for whatever happens is so soulfully important that it deserves a spell and blessing all its own. Give thanks before and after every ritual. In the beginning, we thank the deities stopping by for a spell, and in the end, we're thankful for what happened, even if we don't know what that is. We pray to live lives full of nothing but gratitude. In a soulful gesture of gratitude, works of mercy are called for in "closing" our spells. Donate time or money to the homeless. Visit the sick. Comfort the sorrowful. Counsel the doubtful. Be kind to strangers, who have a biblical reputation of being angels in disguise. Becoming a grateful person is what it means to be divinely human, so gestures of gratitude at the end of every spell become us. Ending full of gratitude, not attitude, is the clearest sign we're given, indicating our prayer is heard and our wish is being granted. Let it be.

BLESSED BE

*If the only prayer you ever say in your
entire life is "thank you,"
it will be enough.*

–Meister Eckhart

AFTERWORD

*E*nding this book with a blessing of thanks is also meant to thank you for joining me in attempting to renew the face of this earth with a reverence for all life and the beliefs of all those who walk this earth with us. I like the thought of Sufi mystics who believe we are all walking each other home. After I finished this book, I felt it took on a life of its own and wasn't mine anymore, sort of like parents whose kids leave home, adding a kind of magic to the life of the book in finding those who seek its message. It is my hope that this book gave you what you needed, led you to what you were looking for, and continues to grant you peace. If it has done all of that, mission accomplished. You now have all you need to find what you're looking for, to grant your wishes, and to become grounded in a kind of peace that cannot be disturbed.

After all is said and done, what remains to be seen is what we can all do with divine intervention to bring joy to the world and peace to this earth. You also have all you need within you to make the kind of magic that transforms darkness into light, confusion into clarity, suffering into well-being, even death into everlasting life. You have all you need within you to bring God into your homes where families are moved to abide in love. And you have all you need to alter the course of events with personal and ritual prayer. We can all make that kind of magic. In my mind, the world is our church, and we are all priests and priest-esses called to bring people together in working for what's best for all. Every day I light a candle for all who've found this book, or all who this book found, thankful for the ties that bind when we become enlightened enough to see how we are all one in this world, called to "walk each other home." My prayer in every word of this book is that "all may be one." So, thank you for finding this book, or letting it find you. Thank you for walking home with me.

ABOUT THE AUTHOR

KAROL JACKOWSKI joined the Sisters of the Holy Cross in South Bend, Indiana in 1964. In 1990, she moved to New York City to finish her PhD at NYU. In 1995, she became part of the Sisters for Christian Community, an independent, self-governing sisterhood. She is the author of numerous books and an acclaimed artist, whose work is in private collections and displayed in the Veselka restaurant in New York's East Village.

TO OUR READERS